Other Titles by Susie Bright

Full Exposure: Opening Up to Your Sexual Creativity and Erotic Expression

The Sexual State of the Union

The Best American Erotica 1993, 1994, 1995, 1996, 1997, 1999, 2000, 2001 (editor)

Nothing But the Girl: The Blatant Lesbian Image
(with Jill Posener)

Herotica, Herotica 2, Herotica 3 (editor)

Sexwise

Susie Bright's Sexual Reality: A Virtual Sex World Reader

Susie Sexpert's Lesbian Sex World

the best
AMERICAN
EROTICA
2001

edited by

Susie Bright

A Touchstone Book
Published by Simon & Schuster
New York London Toronto Sydney Singapore

TOUCHSTONE
Rockefeller Center
1230 Avenue of the Americas
New York, NY 10020

Introduction and compilation copyright © 2001 by Susie Bright

Designed by Joy O'Meara

Manufactured in the United States of America

3   5   7   9   10   8   6   4   2

ISBN 0-684-86914-4

Acknowledgments

Thank you to my father, Bill Bright, for all his editing expertise; to my managers and agents, Joanie Shoemaker and Jo-Lynne Worley; and to my editor at Simon & Schuster, Doris Cooper—for all their work and attention to this collection. I'd also like to thank Jennifer Taillac, Ina Nadborny, Jill Wolfson, and Jon Bailiff for their support.

The Best American Erotica 2001 is dedicated
to my friend Louise Rafkin

Contents

Contents *13*

Introduction

I've never been questioned so closely until now. I've never been treated with such scrutiny and criticism. When I started *The Best American Erotica* series in 1993, the question people asked was, "Where do you find erotic literature?"—as in, "Any source whatsoever." They assumed I had nothing to look at except a bunch of spanky romps signed by "Anonymous" or steamy letters to the editor so prolifically found in pint-size stroke 'zines at the newsstand.

It's true, at that time you could count the number of literary erotic short stories on two hands. I worried that I wouldn't be able to fulfill my contract, which stipulated that the publisher needed at least twenty stories to make a decent page count. I wondered if I would have to write a story myself under a pseudonym, or if I should change the title of our collection from *The* Best *American Erotica* to *The* Only *American Erotica*. I haunted friends and even relative strangers with my quest: "Where are the erotic writers?" I chewed my nails. They had to be out there somewhere—and I felt it in my gut—there must be more than twenty.

Nowadays I face a different sort of question. Readers and critics alike wonder how I can possibly read all the erotica published—and, in particular, how I can keep up with the publishing infinity machine that is called the Internet. In the time it takes me to write this introduction, there are probably one thousand erotic poems, short stories, and novellas being uploaded onto the Web for the very first time—some with great fanfare and others quite obscure. Within minutes, however, all these authors will receive reactions and critiques from around the world; their stories will be quoted, copied, imitated, and even sabotaged by their newfound and greedy public.

My response to the millions of splitting embryos? Thank God for cream, I say. Thank all the erotic muses and laws of literary karma—because the writing that is the very best, the most cherished and deeply influential, does find its way to the top, like the richest cream. If you have any eye for talent at all, you can even see the cherry on top, winking at you.

When people ask me who might be my inspiration, I have to credit a character from the late, great Charles Schulz: Linus, in the Pumpkin Patch. Linus's faith in the rewards of sincerity and passion is my divining rod as well.

Linus believes in the Great Pumpkin, a bountiful magical figure whom the other children scorn or have never even heard of. While all the other kids look to Santa Claus or the Tooth Fairy for their just deserts, Linus looks out to his Pumpkin Patch, where he's been growing his organic best, his squashes watered and tended with infinite love. He hopes the Great Pumpkin will rise up Halloween night, witness his efforts, and reward his sincerity. *Sincerity* is the key word here—the Great Pumpkin knows a poser pumpkin when he sees one, and isn't about to applaud any phony or halfhearted efforts.

From the beginning of my career in erotica, I was told that

no one believed in the idea of a story that was arousing yet literary. The very notion was a contradiction in terms to the "experts." If it gets you off, it's crude smut, they said—and if it's a lovely story, it'll put you to sleep right quick. Women don't want sex in their stories, they smirked; they want romance. Real men don't *read* sex, they laughed, they want four-color layouts with bigger and better Bunnies.

But I knew there was an honest appreciation of the sensuous word, and that sex was too deep in the human character to be exempt from worthy self-expression. If you're alive and breathing, I reckoned, you have a sexual story to tell; and somewhere, someone had to be writing it down, even if it was kept quite secret, and certainly unedited.

I also knew that the small cadre of fans like myself, who believed in the mystical beast of erotic literature, were on a very tight grapevine together, and we supported every tender new shoot that sprung up.

So we kept planting and going public with our harvest. In what must be the fastest-growing fiction genre ever seen, the post-1980s' erotic fiction renaissance broke through decades of censorship and stagnation, and the next generation of erotic originals began to form its own galaxy. Today there are thousands of erotic Web sites, stories, and compendiums; the bookstores that once feared the consequences of putting one erotic book on the shelf now have a whole section, from ceiling to floor.

Nevertheless, the sincerity factor is still rare, and still remarkable. Like other popular phenomena, erotic fiction may have grown to gargantuan proportions, but that doesn't mean that genuine quality has rooted every effort. If you follow Linus's teachings, it's not the *size* of the pumpkin that makes its flesh sweet, and that was never more true than when it came to sex and the word. The Great Pumpkin in the Sky will always see behind the hype and the mass-produced, the flashing cookies and the neon ta-tas.

When I see the plethora of erotic books and Web sites, I say, "Good for them." Good for their initiative, their hard clits and wet pants. But when I read the ingredients on their pages, like any can of soup, their contents often reveal too much artificial junk, without the original taste I'm looking for.

The sad truth about most of what's sold as sex books, sex aids, and sex gurus is that it's fourth-rate slop presented to consumers as something they'll buy because people are just too stupidly horny to expect anything better. Put "SEX" on the cover with a pink ribbon, and watch the suckers fall for it—that's the maxim of many on the erotic publishing scene. It doesn't matter if it's good or sincere; what matters is that you touch the familiar keys, press the prurient buttons, adding salt, adding sugar—leaving you hungry again ten minutes later.

It's not hard for me to single out the outstanding erotica when there is so much cynicism and exploitation in this genre. The artists and publishers who actually give a damn are like angel-flesh glowing under the moonlight—I can see them a mile away, and I want to cut through the muck faster to get close to them. The writers and publishers you see represented in *BAE* are not only erotic, they are exotic, in the sense that their fragrance and meatiness are genuine rarities.

If you love sexual writing and art, you know how false the stereotypes are that surround it—erotic expression is the hardest thing to do well, not the easiest. When I find great erotic writers, I know they could write about death, about violence, about intimacy, about the end of the world and the first gasp of life. Shakespeare wrote his sonnets in a lover's voice, but his words testify to the writer's muse as well: "Being your slave, what should I do but tend upon the hours and times of your desire?" Those hours are well spent, as every sincere devotee can attest. What is the drama of arousal after all, or the comedy of our sexual manners, if not the ground soil of every fiction? I'll take mine fresh, right off the vine.

—Susie Bright
February 2001

the best
AMERICAN
EROTICA
2001

TODD BELTON
Expanding on an Idea

She says she likes my breasts because they're small.

You don't want these, she says. They hurt every day and they make my back hurt too. They bounce around and get in your way and weigh you down.

She likes my breasts because they're small. She says. I love her breasts because they're big.

Sometimes I watch her, sitting at the table across from me. Her with a figure like an pneumatic cartoon, me with the gentle line of an Arp sculpture. I imagine her breasts growing, growing until their weight has made them sag enough to collide with the tabletop. She looks down, puzzled, then drops her fork. Tomato sauce splashes onto the top of her left breast and her neck. I walk around behind her chair, lean in and nuzzle her like a deer, licking it off.

Cut that out, she says, too distracted. Look at my breasts. This is really strange. By now they are more than filling the available space, descending into her lap, the table's edge making a deep dent as they push against and over it. Good thing you're not wearing a bra, I say. Come into the living room, you'd better take that top off while you can.

But—but—I need to get to a hospital, she stammers. This is crazy. What's going on?

Relax, I say. I'm sure they'll go back to normal soon.

I tug on her hand—she stands up and follows, dazed. In the living room, I pull and cajole her T-shirt over breasts it was never designed to contain. She cradles her breasts in her hands and tries to lift them. They spill out over her fingertips. They're still growing, she says. Now that I'm holding them, I can feel it.

Sit down, I say. She sits. I sit next to her. I lean into her lap and put my mouth on the nearer nipple, rolling my tongue over it. She shrieks. Are they sensitive? I say, trying to be innocent.

How can you think about that right now? she asks. Why not? I reply, and lick her nipple again. She squirms and pushes me away. I'm not kidding, she says. This is serious.

She stands, with some effort. While she sat, her breasts had filled her entire lap. Bending forward from the weight, she makes her way over to her room and the table with the telephone.

Who are you calling? I ask. The doctor, who do you think? she replies.

I watch as she stands impatiently, obviously having more and more trouble standing as her breasts continue to swell. If she continues leaning forward at that rate, and they continue growing at the same rate, soon they will reach her knees.

The doctor's office has placed her on hold. She doesn't look happy.

I put a CD in the player, turned low to not interfere with her call. The hole in the CD would fit over her nipple, just snug enough to stay on, like a piece of jewelry. The CD itself would cover her areola, but only barely. I could get one of the two-CD sets out; then they'd match. The *White Album* might look nice.

She thuds behind me and I spin around. She has dropped the phone, gone to her hands and knees, breasts spreading out where they meet the floor like beanbags.

Help me, she says. Get them back on the phone. I can't stand up anymore.

I move to the phone, stand in front of it so she can't see me. With my finger I hang up silently. I speak one-half of an imaginary conversation. The doctor is out. I make it plausible. There is no immediate danger. They will send an ambulance as soon as they can, since the condition is obviously not urgent.

I put the receiver down, turn around and gasp.

What I am looking at is a fair approximation of an earthball with a person lying on top of it. Her feet do not touch the ground. She is floating atop her breasts, arms and feet hanging off, waving ineffectively. I walk around to see her face. She is shaking her head dully, eyes wide and mouth open, in complete disbelief.

She recovers when I work my fingers around her waist, pressing in against ballooned tissue to unfasten her jeans. Hey, she says, what's going on back there?

I'm taking off your pants, I say. I think you'll be more comfortable.

When is the ambulance coming? she asks, and I realize I have probably wasted a good made-up conversation.

When they can get one, I say. It might be a while. They don't think your condition is urgent.

Not urgent? she sputters. I can't move. I can't do anything. What do they consider urgent?

Shhh, I say, rubbing the taut skin of her breasts, one hand to either side of where her legs rest in front of me. How do they feel?

Pretty good, actually—she says, and then she sighs at the feeling as I caress the overtaxed skin.

I gradually manage to get her panties down over her legs and off. I suppose that was to make me more comfortable too, she says wryly.

I don't say anything. I move her legs apart and begin to lick where her cunt is against her breasts, prying my tongue into the narrow space where they're pressed together. She squeaks.

What, you don't like that? I ask. I press one hand into her breasts on either side to steady myself and go in again with my tongue, sliding it up along the sensitive skin of her breasts and then moving directly into her crotch. Poking my tongue in hard to overcome the pressure. She gasps.

Hmm, this is tricky, I say aloud. My tongue is not quite long enough, given the position. Don't go away, I can't resist saying as I walk into the other room.

I get our favorite silicone toy and some lube. Squeezing the dildo in my hands to warm it up, I go back into the living room. She can't see me. I push hard and rock her forward, rolling her like a ball, so that her head tilts down and almost hits the floor. She stops herself with her hands. Hey! she says. Have you lost your mind?

I walk around onto her side and pull her legs up into the air, away from her breasts. Now she almost looks like she's doing a headstand—next to an earthball. I slide the lubed toy into her and she squeaks. What's that for? she asks. You were doing fine on your own.

I rest her legs against her built-in beachball again and roll her back so she's resting atop. How's that feel? I ask.

Wow, she says. Um, my breasts are pressing against it, holding it in.

That's what I thought, I say.

I reach for her butt, squeezing one cheek in each hand gently, and begin to rock her back and forth over the rug. Head almost to the ground, then rock backward until the feet touch the ground on the far side. Back and forth. Her breasts rubbing and brushing against the deep pile rug, and her full pussy caught between the rolling pressure of her own swollen breasts and my hands firmly against her ass.

Back and forth. She begins to gasp every time I push, every time her face rocks forward.

I can stop if you like, you know, I say.

Don't you dare, she pants.

Back and forth. Face forward—exhale loudly—feet back—inhale sharply. She sounds like she's doing Lamaze breathing.

What did you say? I stop suddenly to ask.

Faster, she says faintly.

I put one hand on her ass and another on her spine between the shoulders and begin to rock her as quickly as her size permits. She pants like a locomotive, fast and loud. *Chug chug chug*. Wetness from her cunt is dripping down shinily over the round surface she rests on; I can see it between her slightly spread legs. She is moaning now.

Then, from her mouth, comes the sound a balloon makes when you hold the neck taut as you let the air out. A loud squeak, very high at first but dropping in pitch very fast. And as she makes this noise, as the air rushes out of her, her breasts deflate and she tumbles down to the floor, cushioned in her fall as they rapidly shrink away to normal.

And she is lying facedown, spread on the rug, dripping into it, sweating, exhaling. Her whole body in contact with the carpet again.

She says that big breasts are a real problem. She says I don't want them. Well, goodness, I know that.

I never said I wanted them for myself.

MARGE PIERCY
From *Three Women:*
The New Kid

The first time they had sex, they were stoned and kept giggling. It didn't hurt but it didn't feel like much. They didn't date like the straight kids. Both his parents worked and her mother was always at the law office or in court, so they just fucked whenever they felt like it. When her sister Rachel was home from grade school, Elena took Evan into her room and shut the door. They played music loud. She had Rachel cowed. She knew that even if Rachel suspected anything, she wouldn't tell their mom, Suzanne: she'd be scared to. Evan put on his father's overcoat and went into an adult bookstore. He bought books about sex and several women's videos. After that, he spent an hour looking for Elena's clit, till he found it.

If other girls asked her about him, she said he was like her brother. They were both intense and dark and aloof: even more than her brother or her lover, Evan was like her twin. They liked the same thrash bands; they liked dark violent movies that felt real; they liked taking their clothes off and trying different things. They always did their homework together and they always had sex using condoms. Neither could drive a car, for they were both fourteen. They had to use their bikes or public transportation to go anywhere. They bought their dope in the neighborhood, at a spot outside a drugstore where guys she knew from grade school were selling. Both of them loved their neighborhood, with its blocks that matched, each block a particular type of red brick rowhouse, some with funky little strip gardens in the middle of the street.

Evan and she didn't talk about garbage like love and families. They talked about peace and death and hypocrisy and lies. They did his next science project together and then they let the mice go in the basement of the school. She hoped they could make it on their own.

In school, she was too weird for the other girls. If she stood with a group of girls, conversation slowed down or stopped. She got her breasts and she was tall, so guys were always trying to feel her up, poking at her, making noises, but they were scared of her too and never bugged her about dating. She listened to the other girls talking about their boyfriends, and it wasn't like that with her. She didn't dote on Evan. It was as if they were each other's shadow. He called them E squared or E to the second power. There was no hand holding, no smooching, no rings or pins or flowers. They fought sometimes and called each other names, but it never lasted. They would start laughing as if for them to be anything but one being, one conspiracy, one gang of two, was a joke. She could not even have said if she loved Evan. It was like loving her arm. They were a unit. His parents and hers asked questions, but they had no idea how much time the two of them spent together. Their grades stayed high.

The next year a new student transferred in from Kansas. They both had History with him. He wasn't a jock, a club kid, one of the super-students who ran the school, or a burnout who would be tossed out, but like them, one of the weird kids. He was between them in height and had pale sleek blond hair he wore to his shoulders. His eyes were a dark haunting blue. He had a scar through one light brown eyebrow. His cheekbones were high and sharp and his profile looked to her as if it should be carved on the prow of a sailing vessel. He always had shadows of stubble on his cheeks that made him seem older, more experienced. Half the guys had just started shaving. Evan had a darkish beard but not much of it. He only had to shave every other day and it took him about a minute, although she did like to watch, 'cause it was such a male thing to do. She was almost hairless on her body and never shaved her legs. To each other, they called the new kid the Decadent Viking.

"I want him," Evan said.

"So do I," she said. "We'll share him."

They made up stories of capturing him, tying him up and doing things to him. His name was Chad, a silly name for such a fascinating-looking guy. He was broody. He sat at the back, and even when he knew the answers, he sounded as if he resented being right. She sat down next to him in Assembly one day. His wrists stuck out below his shirt. There was a scar on each of them. He caught her looking at his wrists. He didn't hide them. She stared at him. He stared back. Then he smiled.

For two months they didn't do anything more than make up stories about Chad the Decadent Viking. Then Evan asked him one day, "Want to study for History finals with Elena and me?"

"Is she your girl?"

"I don't even know what that means."

They went over to Evan's house. He didn't have a pesky kid sister, only an older brother who was at William and Mary. For the first hour they studied together up in Evan's room, smoking cigarettes and dope and studying really hard, but Elena knew Evan was planning something. It made her feel tense and excited. She trusted Evan and she didn't care what he did, as long as Chad didn't laugh at them. She got worked up just sitting there knowing that Evan was about to make his move.

He stood up suddenly and came over to her, drawing her to her feet. He began unbuttoning her blouse. "Get undressed, Elena, and lie on the bed."

Chad remained in his chair. "Hey. What's going on?"

"Watch," was all Evan said. He waited till she had stripped and lay on the bed, feeling exposed but also high from the way that Chad was staring at her. She knew that she looked good and that he couldn't turn his eyes away. In the meantime, Evan quickly undressed and grabbed a condom. Then he lay down on top of her. He could tell she was excited already and simply pushed in and began to fuck her. She glanced over at Chad. He was staring at them but he hadn't moved. She loved the feeling of him watching them, as if he were in their power and couldn't break away. She came quickly. So did Evan.

He stood up, not covering himself, and came to stand in front of Chad. He motioned for Elena to come over. Slowly, loose and wet after coming, she obeyed. She almost felt sorry for Chad. Instead of looking cool and in command the way he always did, he looked lost, almost scared, but he stood his ground. She had no idea what Evan was about to do, and in a way she was scared too, but she trusted him. It would be something wild. She thought Evan was enjoying the upper hand and the power to shock Chad.

"Do you want us?"

Chad was so startled he couldn't reply for a moment. Then he repeated, "Us?"

"We come as a set. We don't separate. Or are you scared?"

"I never did it with a guy."

She knew Evan hadn't either, but he wasn't going to say so, and she wouldn't betray him. "Have you ever done it with a girl?"

"Once," Chad said reluctantly. "Almost." His gaze returned to her body. His eyes excited her. Evan never looked at her that way. They were so used to each other's bodies, they took nakedness as a matter of course. But in the year they had been fucking, her body had changed. She had real breasts now, and her behind was curvier. She liked Chad staring at her. Chad raised his gaze to look into her eyes. "Don't you have a will of your own?"

"We're together," Elena said indignantly. "He doesn't make me do what I don't want to. We're honest with each other. Clear."

"Do you love him?" Chad asked.

Elena took a step backward from Chad, shaking back her hair. "I don't know what that means."

Chad grinned narrowly, as if she had given him back a measure of initiative. "But I do."

"If you don't want to, nobody's making you." Elena made as if to reach for her T-shirt from a Hole concert.

He caught her wrist. He gave her a push so she sat down hard on the edge of the bed. Then slowly and deliberately he undid his belt buckle and then his shirt and then his jeans. Evan watched him with his head cocked, smiling slightly.

Chad was erect so he couldn't be that put off. She stared at his cock, because it was only the second one she had ever seen. He looked different from Evan, sort of bigger and looser around the top. "I'm not circumcised," he said. "My father doesn't believe in it."

Evan straddled his desk chair, keeping out of the way. Elena waited until Chad had undressed completely and sat on the bed's edge next to her. Then without waiting for him to make a move, she slid toward him and, taking his face in her hands, gave him a sensuous tongue kiss. She moved her thigh against his. She wanted him so badly she ached. She did not think she had ever wanted Evan this strongly, but she would never let him know that. It would hurt his feelings, and he was her own. Her flesh. Her more-than-brother.

Chad's hand was on her breast now, a little awkwardly, squeezing hard. With Evan she would have instructed him, but she couldn't risk discouraging Chad. They had wanted him and now they were going to have him, both of them. Now he was lying on top of her, kissing her almost frantically. She slid a rubber on his prick with both hands and guided him in. Normally she would have liked fooling around with him longer, but she did not want anything to go wrong. He thrust hard and came almost at once, long before she could. Then he lay spent on the bed, while she eased out from under him.

Evan let him lie like that for several minutes. Then he motioned for her to get up. She took the desk chair, which Evan had dragged to just beside the bed to watch more closely. Evan lay down beside Chad. At first he just caressed him from the back, making spoons. Evan's chest and pubic hair were dark, almost black, and Chad's body hair was the palest brown. Chad was tanned over his arms and chest. Evan was milky pale. Evan patiently caressed Chad, reaching around to his cock. Then he rolled Chad onto his stomach, rolled on another condom, and, using the surgical jelly he had stashed under the bed, slowly, caressing his way, put himself into Chad's ass. Chad winced and bit at the pillow, but once Evan was in, he seemed to mind it far less. She liked watching. She loved watching. She was possessing Chad through Evan's cock. She was fucking him through Evan. She wanted Evan to thrust harder, but he was careful, gentle. She could almost feel his come. Then he rested for a moment, turned Chad over and began to suck his cock.

Afterward Chad lay as if dazed. "Do you do this a lot?" he asked finally, trying to recover himself.

"We fuck all the time," Evan said. "We study and we fuck. But it's the first time we've taken anybody else with us. You should consider it an honor." He was grinning widely.

"Oh, I do."

"Did you like being with us?" Elena asked almost shyly. He was so beautiful, Chad with the blue blue eyes and the carved face.

"I've spent worse afternoons." He reached out and pulled her down on the bed with him. He was staring into her eyes. "I don't understand you."

"Sometimes I don't understand myself."

With a light caress now his hand moved over her breast. "You're like something I made up lying in bed at night."

Evan said, "You know, we could all have a lot of fun."

Chad looked at him, his hand coming to rest on Elena's bare thigh. "I think you're right."

CARA BRUCE
You Know What?

work in a place "nice girls" don't usually visit. Starting about four in the afternoon I enter a black covered doorway underneath a flashing marquee that reads "LIVE GIRLS — ALL NUDE." I am a performer, a dancer, an exhibitionist. And I like it.

Sometimes I strip onstage but mostly I work the booths. The booths in my joint have a tiny bit of glass at the bottom but besides that they are open so I can see everything the John is doing, and he can see me. If a girl wants to make some extra money she can let the guys touch, there is also a security button if they get out of control.

I like it this way. I like to watch the men jerking off. I like to look right in their eyes as I shake my tits and move my shaved pussy up and down in front of their faces. Some girls hate to know what the customers are doing, but not me. I'm causing it, therefore I own the reaction. I want to know what I own. This is why I make the most money.

I don't usually let anyone touch, I just like the watching. Just the two of us, making each other hot as hell, with me using no hands, only motions, in a space as big as my bathroom closet.

One day I was working the booths, it was pretty slow. A couple of guys had come in, one just sat there, staring at me. I don't like it when they just look. I want participation. Makes me feel as if I'm doing a better job. One guy jerked off, came in about two strokes. Made me feel as if I were doing too good a job. Then this woman comes in. Now sometimes we get lesbians or prostitutes with dates, and once in a while there are girls that come in with their boyfriends. Usually these women won't even look at me, they look at the floor, their feet, their boyfriend, or try and make out to distract themselves from the show. It's like they're embarrassed for themselves and for me. I always try to dance harder to force their attention. The couples never stay long.

So anyway, this woman comes in. She is hot, I look at her, dressed in her chic black business suit, little skirt, blouse, and matching jacket. And the first thing I think is that she might be a cop, but she sits down and puts some quarters in. The lights come on and I can hear a faint beat of music from whoever is dancing outside, so I start to grind my hips and toss my hair.

The woman stares right at me, as if she's daring me to show her what I've got. So I do. I look right back in her eyes and start fucking an imaginary body, real slow and sensual like. And she keeps looking. She drops more quarters in and she spreads her legs.

She's not wearing anything underneath, and I wonder if she

went to work like this. Her legs are spread wide and she's shaved bare as well, giving her big and thick lips plenty of air. Now I'm thinking maybe she's in the business, and I start sort of showing off for her.

I bring my cunt down right in front of her face, and you know what she does? She breathes on it. Real hot breath coming out and almost making me lose my balance. So I keep dancing, grinding real close to her face. She starts unbuttoning her blouse, no bra on. She lets her tits fall out, then she starts rubbing and pinching her own nipples.

She's trying to outdo me, I think. I shake my head, that bitch is trying to steal my spotlight. So I reach down by my feet and I pick up my prop, a big pink vibrator. I'll give her something to feel herself about all right. I take the toy and draw it slowly through my mouth, lubing it up. She licks her lips, still staring right into my eyes. I bring the vibrator down and tease my clit with it, knowing it'll pop out hard and full, giving her something to stare at. So I start moving the vibrator around, turning it up a notch and breaking a sweat.

She has her skirt around her waist now, her long legs spread wide. She tilts her hips up and starts jilling off.

She mimics me, each stroke I make with my vibrator she copies with her finger. It's a masturbation duel and I'm not sure if the objective is to come first or last. Without missing a beat she puts more quarters in.

I slide the vibrator up inside me. She matches this with her fingers. I'm squatting, using my palm to stick the vibrator up, then releasing my muscles to let it fall back. Her digits are diving in and out, with the same gentle rise and fall. I shake my head, I'm on fire now, this woman is making me hot. Her pretty head is tilted back slightly, her lips parted, her eyes stuck on mine.

Suddenly it hits me. I want to fuck her. I don't usually do customers, but I want her real bad. I get up in her face, my whirring cunt is inches from her mouth, and I say, "You want me."

She smiles, her hand never stops, and she says, *"You want me."*

"Fuck me," I tell her, and my voice quivers a little with the excitement, even though I'm trying to sound stern.

She takes the vibrator in her mouth, and she starts fucking me with it. I'm squatting above her and she is fucking me with my own vibrator in her mouth. Meanwhile, her hand never stops moving. She's getting lipstick all over my toy and juices from my dripping slit are sliding down and gathering on the corners of her red lips and she is still staring at me. My legs are trembling, because she is fucking the hell out of me and herself at the same time.

"Yeah, honey, fuck me, fuck me," I pant, and I can almost see her smile.

I wrap my hands around her head and push her deeper into me. I'm moving her head and every time I look down those eyes are staring at me. My legs are shaking and my cunt starts to clench and I feel my insides begin to boil and I look down and she winks at me. I can't believe it, I lose my shit. I start to come, shaking and crying I fall over on her.

"Please stop, stop, stop," I cry, but she won't. That vibrator isn't moving but it's still deep inside me. I reach down to grab her hair but then, the bitch, she starts to come and I get off again, just feeling her shaking and moaning under me. It's too much.

She's done, and finally she pulls out the vibrator. I climb off of her and she turns off the toy and places it down on the little stage. I'm spent, I feel like I've been fucked for the first time in a long time, and if the floor wasn't covered with spent jizz, maybe I could crawl up and go to sleep there.

She's still looking at me, that smile that's more like a smirk on her face, and she's buttoning up her blouse and pulling down her skirt. She stands up, looking like nothing ever happened and she walks over and you know what she does? She kisses me. Plants a big wet one right on my mouth while she slides a twenty on the stage then she turns and walks out.

I can't believe her. The nerve of that slut, I know her type, the kind that always needs the last word. I shake my head, some people are just crazy, you know what I mean? I get back onstage and wait for my next show.

MATT BERNSTEIN SYCAMORE
Sink

My eyes rolled back and I was looking in the mirror the way I used to look at people late late *late* at clubs when the drugs were taking me to that planet I never wanted to leave. But this time it was just me and the bathroom sink. That's when our relationship began. Two months and still going strong; it's the second-longest relationship I've ever had. And this one doesn't have *any* of the drama.

He's kind of falling apart, but he's dependable. And beautiful, in the way that only a sink can be beautiful. *And* he's got character. This isn't some Formica mess from the seventies, with square edges and gold glitter. And it's not one of those sinks that look all glamorous from a distance, but then you get up close and the drain's rusted shut, the faucets are about to break off. This sink is the real thing, made during the forties.

You know, the golden years. Sure, he's seen a little wear and tear, but haven't we all. I mean, I'm only twenty-four and I've got suitcases under my eyes.

It all started one night after a trick. He wanted me to fuck him hard, harder, and after a few thrusts it actually started turning me on. I was pounding him as hard as I could and he was grabbing my ass to pull my dick in farther. That got me to relax. I mean, I don't like fucking someone really hard unless I know he's enjoying it. So I put my hands on his back and got into a good rhythm, sliding my dick almost all the way out then shoving it back in as far as it would go. It got to the point where his moans and my grunts were synchronized, which kind of put me in a trance. I think I even heard my balls slapping against his ass like in some porn video.

I could feel myself getting close to coming, so I stopped and held my dick all the way in his ass, but I started spasming anyway. Usually, I don't like to come with guys who are paying me, and there's nothing worse than coming when I'm trying not to. It's like doing bad drugs, makes me tense instead of euphoric. But somehow this time I managed to hold it in, even though I thought for a second that I could feel my cum spilling into the condom. Either the trick thought I was coming too or our bodies were really in tandem, which would be kind of scary. But anyway he started gasping and then he moved forward quickly and my dick slid out. And then he came. I was covered in sweat, so I took a shower while he called a taxi.

Got home and I was exhausted. Then of course I got horny. I always get horny when I think I'm too tired to move. I couldn't stop thinking about fucking some sweaty guy with a shaved head and a firm body, pounding his asshole and digging my fingers into the groove between his chest muscles until we came at the same time. He'd reach back and grab my ass to keep my dick in his asshole longer, my arms around him, tongue reaching for the back of his throat. I got hard just thinking about it, the kind of hard that makes me think my dick might explode. Not like when I'm about to come, but like *Isn't this thing too red?*

I went into the bathroom to watch myself jerk off in the mirror. My dick was so hard it was vibrating. I pulled off my shirt and grabbed my armpits, licked the mirror in circles like I was making out with someone, or maybe just to see what it would taste like. The mirror got all foggy. I spit on my hand and started pumping my dick into both my fists, trying to watch myself while licking one of my armpits, which was tastier than the mirror.

I remembered Greg calling me up one night to tell me shea butter was the best lube, so I rubbed some between my hands and then onto my dick, started thrusting my dick against the rounded top of the sink, without hands. I pulled the shea butter back out of the cabinet and rubbed it onto the sink. Felt great, but the sink still wasn't slippery enough. I opened the cabinet again and took our some of this sticky vitamin E lotion that I use as pomade. Then I went into the other room and got some Bodywise Silk, the British lube that feels like lotion, and I mixed all three together.

My dick felt harder than rock-hard (granite-hard? marble-hard?). I looked in the mirror and my face was what my mother used to call lobster-red. Started pushing down on my dick so there was more friction. Sliding all the way out past the cock head and then back toward the faucet. Each time my dick slipped off the sink, I'd jerk off until I could tell by the look on my face that I was about to come, then I'd grab the sink with my hands and start pumping faster. I wanted to come without using my hands, like my dick was in someone's ass and I was pulling him against me. I got really close and then my dick slipped off again. I started pounding the sink as hard as I'd been pounding that trick, my thighs making noise—more noise than before—because porcelain echoes.

It felt good to squeeze the sink with my thighs, balancing my weight on top and thrusting hard. Concentrating to keep my dick from slipping off. Pushing down on my dick with my hands so I'd get closer to coming. By this time I was moaning, pounding the sink and sweating. And then I slipped again. Held my dick and smacked it against the sink until it felt as stiff as the sink (sink-hard). Then I grabbed on to the sides of the sink with my hands and pushed on the front with my thighs, thrusting fast now. Hard and fast and then sliding slowly back until my cock almost slipped off, then pounding again. I was concentrating so hard that I didn't even think of fantasizing. Thrusting my dick faster and faster, and when I came I felt like I'd split apart.

It sure feels sexy to squeeze my thighs up against that sink. The sink feels so strong, I can trace the rough spots where the enamel's chipped, but I know the sink's not going to break. Even if there are some dark areas and the white is fading to yellow. This sink was built to last, I can press down with all my weight and it doesn't even budge. That's firmer than any guy's six-pack.

Let me tell you that the sex I have with my sink is a lot better than most of the sex I've had with other guys. My sink's not going to tease my asshole with his dick, then slide it in without a condom. Or leave in the morning before I even have a chance to say good-bye. Sure, I wish the sink were more responsive, but you can't have everything, right?

Okay, maybe you think I'm in denial about the fact that when I'm having sex with my sink, I'm really masturbating.

So if you want me to use the word *masturbation,* I'll use it. Let's just call it masturbation with a partner. I mean, plain old masturbation was never this exciting. I don't always fuck the sink, that's for special occasions. But I love to press the shaft of my dick against the top of the sink while I grab my abs with one hand and my balls with the other. And sometimes I lean against the sink while I slide a dildo into my ass. I can feel the sink warming against my thighs.

I always used to press my dildo against the wall and then slide onto it, but now I've got lots of variations. The other day I put the dildo up on the sink, stood on the edge of the bathtub, and sat on the dildo. I watched myself right up against the mirror. I could see my facial muscles relax as I got closer to coming. Then when I came, I shot all over myself and almost fell into the sink, which was funny and almost romantic. Usually, though, I shoot right into the drain and then just wash my cum down. Though now the drain's starting to clog. And I can't seem to get that vitamin E lotion off the edge of the sink; even when I wash with soap it still feels a bit slimy. (My friends are going to read this and they're going to want to use the kitchen sink, but oh well.)

The view is one of the most important parts. When I'm jerking off in the sink, I'm right up against the mirror. Sometimes I can pretend that I'm watching that Warhol movie I've never seen, the one that's just Joe Dallesandro jerking off from the waist up. I can watch all the different expressions on my face, study my eyes. Watch my jaw clench or slacken as I come and my eyes roll back.

The sink makes me feel good about myself. There's nothing getting in the way of my body becoming my own object of desire. I look in the mirror and think, Who's that hot boy? I tease my tits until they pop up, bite my armpits, smack my chest as hard as I can and watch the red marks as they fade. That first time I fucked my sink, I realized how butch I get when I'm about to come: my face curls up almost into a snarl and I start groaning like some fuck track.

I've been working out and I can watch my body developing. Balancing my hard-on against the sink, I study my new muscles. How hard are the pecs? Are my biceps still bigger than my triceps? I stand up on the toilet so I can see my legs, bend over to look at my ass. Rubbing my hand down over my abs, feeling the hills and valleys as I move from one muscle to another. All the while grinding my dick and getting hornier and hornier. For myself.

It's funny—now I start to get horny every time I'm standing in front of the sink. When I'm shaving, I press forward and I get hard. I'm moving to New York soon, though, and I'm worried that my new sink just won't be the same. It couldn't be this good. And what if I get a sink with sharp edges?

TSAURAH LITZKY
Greek Sex

When Dick Sargent asked me if I ever had Greek sex, I thought he meant did I ever do it with a Greek guy. George Patsakos and I came close to doing it, but George wouldn't fuck me because he and Eddie were both Ravens and I was Eddie's girl. Later, I wished George had fucked me because he was a sweetheart and a turtledove, while Eddie was a sadist and a wastrel under his James Dean mask. I was wilder than either of those guys but I didn't know it then.

I was only sixteen when Dick Sargent asked me the Greek sex question. When I told him I never had any Greek boyfriends, he laughed, then he said, "No, Greek sex is when I put it in your ass."

I was shocked. "How can you get it in there?" I wanted to know. "It must really hurt."

"You inch it in slowly," he said. "If you inch it in slowly, a little bit at a time, it will hardly hurt at all. It's a special way of getting close to someone, and I want to get close to you like that."

I was curious to know what it would feel like to do something so weird, but I wouldn't do anything with Dick Sargent. I didn't like him; he had an ugly tattoo of a skull on his arm that said *Killer,* and he left his wife, Connie, and their baby son, Alex, home all the time while he hung out in the bars. I said no to him, and then he started chasing Judy Starkie and they became lovers. I'm sure he did it with her because whenever I ran into them at the Tip-Toe Inn, he always went out of his way to come over and say hello to me, wearing this shit-eating grin. He would leave her sitting at the bar, chewing on the straw in her rum and Coke. Maybe he imagined my ass-hole when he was poking hers.

After that I started up with Sam, the Quaalude man. He liked to put raspberry jam on his finger and stick it in my ass while we were fucking; he would sniff it after because he liked the combo smell of raspberry jam and bunghole. He taught me to stick my finger up his ass while I blew him (raspberry jam optional). I was trying to get up the courage to ask him to do Greek sex when he got busted selling 'Ludes in the junior high school yard, wearing a nurse's uniform. They sent him away for five years.

Then I met this Greek guy, Tony Vargas from Bath Beach, in a pizza parlor. He liked me to sit on him on a chair and I liked it too. He used to suck at my tits for hours and drive me wild. Once, while he was doing that, I said to him, "Do me the Greek sex way." He jumped up, pulling his thick lips off my nipples.

"That's for whores," he said, "you're a nice girl."

After that he didn't call me, so I took up with Mike Zimmer because there was a rumor that Mike's testicles were as big as lemons. It was true. I sucked those lemons down. I puréed them. I made them into meringue pie and we ate that pie together. One time I asked him if he had ever done Greek sex, and he said yes, but only with men. Then I said, "So, if I'm the first woman you ever do it with, and you're the first man I do it with, we'll be Greek-sex heterosexual virgins together," and he said, "Yes, oh yes." He got the Vaseline out of the bathroom and carried me to the bed. He laid me on my side and coated up my asshole with the Vaseline. He put Vaseline all around and up his index finger and he put it in my asshole. He started an in-out motion and then he leaned over and teased the nipple of my breast with his tongue until I was so wet, my juices rolled out of me onto the sheet. He pulled me up into doggy position and stuck his cock in my ass. There was a little tearing, a little blood, enough for a sacrifice, and then the Snake Goddess Kundalini, with her rainbow scales and crown of baby cobras, rose up out of the blood running down my leg. We danced before her as she flicked her fiery, forked tongue over our writhing limbs. The Tree of Life grew out of her single, shining eye, filling Mike's bedroom with the rustling of Karma Leaves and the fragrance of lotus blossoms.

Mike and I stayed together a couple months but we didn't fall in love, even with the Greek sex; we drifted apart, then we became pals. He married my friend Melanie from Max's, and I don't know what happened to them. Once in a while, a sensitive, ardent practitioner of Greek sex has crossed my path. It was always icing on the cupcake. Now, because of HIV, no one wants to do Greek sex anymore, even with a condom. I know that's for the best, but sometimes I lie awake after the man is sleeping. I put my hand between my legs, stroke my anus, and try to remember the face of the Snake Goddess with her bliss-filled, shining eye.

NATHAN ENGLANDER
From "Peep Show"

Allen Fein is on his way to Port Authority when he stubs his toe and scuffs his shoe—puts a nick in a five-hundred-dollar investment. He pulls out a handkerchief and spit-shines his toe cap, cursing with every pass of the cloth.

The scuffing, the nick, has bumped Allen from the flow to which he is accustomed. And he looks around Forty-second Street at the gentrified theaters and the wholesome shops, the kind a family can enter in the bright light of day. Where are all the hucksters who used to stand outside promising nirvana and shaken booty, forbidden acts and creamy thighs? So busy has Allen been with his own transformation that he's missed the one going on around him.

He blushes at the thought, wondering how little Ari Feinberg had ever become Allen Fein, Esq., in fancy oxblood wingtips. When had he become a grown man, on his way home to a loving wife, a pregnant wife, a beautiful blond Gentile wife, who laughed when he didn't know how to work the Christmas lights, who bought a candle with a picture of Jesus on it when it came time for the memorial for his father? ("They were out of the little white ones," Claire had said. "Can't you just turn Jesus toward the wall?")

Allen straightens his tie and picks up his briefcase. He takes another look around and asks himself: As polished, as straight, as on the up-and-up as Forty-second Street now appears, is it still the same inside?

And then the man says it.

"Buddy," he says. "Mac," he says. "Upstairs. Girls. Live girls inside."

"What?" Allen says, catching the sign in the window: a giant neon token with "25¢" flashing in its center.

"That's right, buddy," the man says. "Twenty-five cents for a spherical miracle. New York's only three-hundred-and-sixty-degree all-around stage. Just follow the stairs, you can't get lost—all the arrows lead to one place."

And Allen goes in, glancing only for a second to see if fate has mustered an officemate or neighbor to descry his ascent. He heads into a stairwell and makes his way to the second floor.

When he enters the hall, he faces a towering figure behind a podium. Behind this giant, the hallway opens into a large room containing a single, massive, pillarlike structure, with doors to individual booths spaced evenly all around.

Allen smiles at the man as if the two were in on a joke, as if his visit were an understandable bit of mischief, the kind of thing he could tell Claire about. Yes, if he feels guilty enough he'll tell Claire he went inside. Allen fishes out a quarter and places it on top of the podium.

"A dollar," the man says.

"It says a quarter."

"It's a dollar," the man says. He does not return Allen's smile.

Fumbling with his wallet, Allen pulls out a five-dollar bill and takes five tokens—too bashful to ask for change.

⑥

"Touch," she says. She is looking right at him, she can see him. This is not how Allen Fein remembers past visits, not with the women staring back. There are four women seated on a carpeted platform, and all, eying him, make the same offer. "Touch," they say. "Touch." Well, three of the women say it. The fourth—sitting in a cheap plastic lawn chair, too wide for it, her thighs, cut in half, drooping, like her breasts, in languid arcs toward the floor—is reading a book. She's got glasses on and is holding a page, ready to turn it, and Allen knows the motion will be slow and lazy, as weary as her posture.

They are all naked, or almost so. The second woman wears a bra, the third panties, and the fourth has the book and glasses. It is the first one who is, to Allen, beautiful.

He has not set foot in a peep show since boyhood, but he recalls almost everything from then. He remembers shivering so badly that his teeth chattered, his hands pressed between his legs for warmth. He'd been afraid that he might freeze to death, actually expire from excitement. And he'd often indulged this nightmare, squandered precious viewing time on the darker fantasy of dropping dead right there in the booth. Allen remembers the old setup. The sound of a token dropping and then the labored spin of gears. He remembers the strip of light at the bottom of the window frame as the wooden partition was drawn up into the wall. Behind thick glass—smudged and fingerprinted, always fogged with heavy breath—were the women. They danced as if they cared, moving to titillate the observer.

The individual booths are more or less the same. It's the windows that are different. Allen is shocked to find that the glass is gone. The women just sit on their chairs, vivid, looking back.

The stage is circular and completely surrounded by the inner wall of the booths. Many of the partitions are raised, and Allen can see men in their compartments at all angles. One middle-aged, broad-headed voyeur is clearly masturbating with vigor. Allen catches the eye of a Latino man off to the side, wearing the very same tie he is. Allen puts a hand to his chest and feels the tie pulsing along with his heart. The Latino man, such a good-looking man, turns away from Allen and makes eye contact with the woman in the bra.

She stands up and walks over to the man and his hands come out through the window, penetrating the fantasy world. Allen has never seen it broached before—the world of dreams cracked open.

When the first girl looks at Allen he feels unworthy to watch. He can hardly bear having her acknowledge him. He wants to ask her what she is staring at. "Can I help you?" he would have said if they were anywhere else. The girl is perfection and Allen wants her desperately. It's a feeling so pure that he wants to cry. How terribly unfair that his whole self aches because of the shape of a shoulder, the soft lines of a hip. Allen stares at the girl's legs, a deep black against the whiteness of the chair, and then up at the trained beckoning in her face. There is the glow of real personality behind the staged.

"Touch," she says. And Allen wants to touch her—to see if she is real. But he hasn't yet responded, and the girl is moving toward him, long and graceful, the woman of his dreams.

Allen is shaking again, as he did when he was a boy. And why shouldn't he? A loyal husband, who, reaching out, touching, had always honored his vows. He does not move his hands or his fingers, just holds them against her wonderful skin, so warm, almost hot. The girl takes Allen's hands in her own, presses them to her chest, and massages. It calms him. She does this like an expert, a masseuse, someone trained in an art. Allen hasn't been so aroused in years. He wants to climb through the small window to be with this woman. But the partition starts to come down. His time has run out. In the split second that he has to make his choice, Allen takes back his hands.

Leaning up against the wall in a panic, Allen tells himself that the fondling of this woman was an aberration, just like his coming up those stairs.

He had only wanted a peep. He'd gone up the stairs a loyal husband and lover, a working man on his way home to the 'burbs. And now, minutes later, a different man emerges: a violator of girls and wives and matrimonial bonds. Allen considers leaving the booth, though his legs feel hollow and unsteady. And there is also his erection, diabolically hard, bringing to mind all the basest descriptions in pornographic magazines.

Allen is so close to climax that he is afraid to move. He wants to get away without having to face the enormity of his pleasure. He remains still, his hand clutched tightly around the tokens, and thinks of Claire waiting at the bus stop, the seat belt stretched over the arc of her stomach, a chamomile tea steaming in her travel mug. But then there is the girl on the other side. So wonderful. Her legs and skin. The way, the skill with which she touched. The idea of her is so enticing it pushes him past control. Allen lets go and lets the shame rush in and fill the emptiness, so that even his hollow legs feel solid and full.

Immediately there is plotting. Already the deceit grows. What to do with his boxer briefs? And to ride the bus to Parsippany this way, to face Claire, soiled. She could drop him at the gym. The gym before dinner, that is the plan. But his erection endures. Allen is neither so old that it should disappear in an instant nor so young that it should remain, and in such a pronounced and steadfast state.

Then again, he thinks, why should it fade when that angel of a girl is so near and there are four more tokens and he has already crossed the threshold and made his way inside? The erection builds strength and, Allen fears, may never go away. He cannot walk out in this state. And he admits to himself that if he didn't ever have to leave, if it meant irretrievably losing the outside world, he would sacrifice it all if only that siren would stand up from her chair, take his hands, and guide them over her body once more. But he won't allow himself such an indulgence. He will put in the token, but he will not touch. He will look at his shoes and the scuff mark that damned him. This is how he will occupy himself, without a whit more enjoyment. He will use up what he paid for, but the penance begins right now.

GINU KAMANI
Waxing the Thing

When I first came to Bombay to work in a beauty salon, I didn't understand anything. They told me to wax, so I waxed: legs, arms, underarms, stomachs, foreheads, fingers, toes. It's like a game for me. I cover the skin of the ladies with hot wax, then quickly-quickly take it all off with a cloth, almost before they notice that it's there. It reminds me of my village school, where I used to draw on the wall with chalk, then quickly wipe it off before the teacher found out. For me it's all very strange, what goes on with these rich-rich city ladies, but I mind my own business. I'm just a simple village girl. Everything about the city is strange to me, so what's one thing more?

There I was, minding my own business, when one day this Mrs. Yusuf, whose legs I was waxing in the private room, asked me if I would come to her house to wax her *thing*. I was so stupid, I asked her to her face, "What is this *thing*?"

Now, she was already lying there with her sari pulled up to her stomach, and her legs bent at the knees, and I was trying not to look at her big white panties that she was shamelessly showing me through her wide-open legs, when suddenly she stuck one finger inside of her panties and pulled the material down and showed me all her hair *there*. I felt so ashamed! All this time, I didn't know that the ladies wax down there.

This Mrs. Yusuf said, very sweetly, that only young girls like me are pure enough in the heart to wax it down there. Naturally she wanted me to go to her house to do this delicate job. In a salon, anyone can walk into the private room, even when the curtain is pulled. Some of the other waxing girls told me that they don't do such type of work. Why shouldn't I? If they want to pay better than at the salon and, on top of that, pay for my taxi here and there, then what do I care.

So I did the work for Mrs. Yusuf, and she told her friends, and before I knew it I had more work waxing things than arms and legs and all. All the ladies like me better because I'm not married. They tell me that marriage will make me rough, like a man, and then I won't be able to do the delicate job.

All our Indians, you know, are so rough and hairy. The shameless Indian men are always scratching themselves between the legs because of the Bombay heat, but the ladies don't have to, because their skin down there is cool and clean. And definitely the smell is also a little less.

I never knew how many kinds of smells could come out of these city ladies' things! Even though they wash night and day and remove every single hair from their bodies, I tell you, some of them smell down there like an armpit. I tell them to put a little baby powder, or maybe even some eau de cologne on the day that I'm coming, otherwise I have to breathe through my mouth so the smell won't drive me crazy. I never used to notice such smells before, but day in and day out putting wax between their legs, I can't help it, my nose has become very nosey.

I'm not so nosey that I ask them questions or anything, but these ladies tell me anyway about why they like to be waxed down there. These thin-thin ladies like Mrs. Nariman and Mrs. Dastur say that it makes them feel clean, because there's no hair for anything to get stuck to down there. Then the gray hair ladies like Mrs. Patel and Mrs. Loelka say it makes them feel like innocent little girls again, and they even talk with giggly, high voices. But worst of all are the lazy, fat ones like Mrs. Singh and Mrs. Vaswani, who tell me it's so much better than getting a massage, giving so much more energy to the body, keeping the blood going all day and all night.

Mostly I don't listen to what they say, but one lady, Mrs. D'Souza, told me a very sad story. She said that she was married so many years, and her husband never liked to do the man's work in her and so they had no children. Finally she got angry and asked him what was wrong with him and he said that it was all her fault, that the hair on her thing was so rough that it poked like pins right into his skin so he couldn't come near her. Poor man! Since then this lady makes me wax her thing every week, even when I can't find one single hair. The whole time, she lies there saying prayers to Mother Mary. At least these days someone like Mrs. D'Souza can wax. In olden days what must have happened to these poor ladies?

My mother in the village still lives like in olden times. I tried to explain to her that I do waxing to make money, but she just can't understand. She stays in the house all day, covered from head to toe in her cotton sari, so how will she understand? These city ladies are not like that. They understand everything, or how else would they all get rich-rich husbands?

My poor mother—it's so shameful—doesn't even wear panties. And she sits with her legs wide open. All the old women are like that. They're so shameless, they don't even *want* to wear anything down there. Without panties, how can a modern girl control her monthly mess? When my mother was young and she got her monthly bleeding, she just sat in one corner and spread this mud between her legs until it mixed with the blood and became hard, a lid made of clay to close her upside-down, bleeding "pot." When she stood up, the hard clay cut into her skin like a knife. For five days she was like that, sitting in one corner with a pile of mud, playing with herself like a mad girl. After the five days, when she tried to break the mud, the hair from down there would be stuck in it and she would pull the hair right off. How she would scream! My god, you would think it was the end of the world. Why such a big fuss over a few hairs? That's the difference, I tell my mother, between her and the big ladies. If she knew what was good for her, she would have pulled *all* the hair out.

The ladies definitely want all their hair out. They make me check again and again for even one single hair that I missed. It's not so easy, you know, unless I shine a torch on it, and anyway, who says I want to look down there? In the beauty salon they told us, if you're plucking a lady's eyebrows, don't look into her eyes; if you're threading her upper lip, don't look into her mouth; so if I'm waxing the thing, I don't look inside there!

Of course, it's my job to get all the hair out, but I can't help it, sometimes the hair just won't come out. I try once or twice, but these fussy ladies are never satisfied. For half an hour I have to feel around bit by bit for any leftover hair, and then even if I find it, how can I wax just one hair? So I have to try to pull it out with my fingers, but even that is impossible because by then the skin has become all sensitive and slippery and sliding.

That Mrs. Yusuf, my god, the way she shouts! "I can feel it, I can feel one hair, not there, other side, in the front, no, no, feel properly, grab the skin with one hand and pull with the other, try again, just wipe your fingers if they're sliding, don't think you can rush away without finishing your job," and on and on. What to do? I don't like digging around in there because I know it's where babies and all come from. But I don't grumble because the fussy ladies always give a good tip. Thank god they are not all like that, or I would have to spend the whole day waxing and cleaning the thing of just one of them!

Not that they are in any hurry. They can just lie there all day, I tell you. At least I don't have to work at night, because the ladies only like me to wax during the day. I have to finish before the husband comes home, because the man doesn't like his wife to be locked in a room with some outsider.

Sometimes when there is a new lady who wants me to go over to do her waxing, she will ask, "How do I know that you will do a good job? It requires such talent, and if you do anything wrong, I'll have to go straight to the hospital." So first I give the new lady the names of some other ladies that I work for, so they can call and find out. And then I tell her that I wax my own thing, not just others', so there's no need to worry. All of them, when they hear this, are so shocked! I'm just a poor village girl, so what do I need to wax for? As though you have to be rich to do it! Am I not a woman like them? Can't I be beautiful like them? If my own sister's husband likes it, then won't mine also want it?

I went back to my village for my oldest sister's marriage, and just to teach her how ignorant she is, I took some wax and clean cloths, and I waxed her. What a fuss that stupid girl made! I had to sit on top of her so she wouldn't run away. But then after the wedding, everyone in the village tells him he's lucky to have such a clean, high-class woman. Until I return, my sister is pulling the hair out from down there one by one with her fingers.

Everyone has something that they can wax, so why not me? I only wax myself once in a while. It's not so easy for me. To wax down there, since I can't bend down to see properly, I have to sit on a mirror. Who would think I would ever look at my own thing? Even all those big-big ladies never look at their thing . . . and me, I've seen so many dozens by now.

"Don't wax it yet, you're not married!" the ladies keep saying. "You're still thin and pure and innocent, and you're not prepared like a married woman for what happens down there. You'll start feeling wrong feeling between your legs, and then no man will take a chance with you. That's why we don't let our unmarried daughters wax down there." I tell you, these ladies think they know everything. I am going to have a love marriage, and I have enough money saved so that I can give a good dowry. What husband will say no to that?

The real reason these ladies don't allow their young daughters to wax down there is because then the daughters will want to have love marriages! And then all the life's work for these rich-rich ladies will go to waste, because if Indian girls are allowed to marry whichever man they want, then who will marry the ladies' good-for-nothing sons? They're very clever, these rich ladies. But very stupid also. They force their daughters to be beautiful so they can arrange a match with a rich boy, but in the end they are marrying off their girls to boys who are exactly the same as their fathers, who make this and that excuse and don't touch one finger to their wives who are waxed clean and ready from head to toe.

So every day, there is plenty of business for the beauty salon, giving these ladies manicures, pedicures, facials, waxing, hair cut, massage. . . . And then some simple village girl like me will come along who doesn't know anything, and they will cunningly find some way to get her to wax their thing. And when they feel something down there which makes them feel like human beings, then they're happy.

But who wants to listen to what I have to say? So I keep my mouth shut and do my work. When the time comes to get married, I will have saved enough money so my husband can treat me well. Until then, I am living without worries, so what do I care?

JOE MAYNARD
Fleshlight

I'm not sure whether or not it's a dubious honor that Ms. Porn Magazine Editor asked me to test-drive a tasty little item called the Fleshlight, but what hooked me was her telling me that the inventor spent two million dollars developing the thing. It's amazing that a budget normally reserved for the space program or the Pentagon was funneled into a sex toy, but whatever. Capitalism minus the cold war, I guess. Figuring that guys like tools, the inventor designed the stealth exterior to look like a flashlight. But inside, Ms. Editor tells me, the tactile matter is damn near identical to the texture of actual labia and vulva flesh: the mother-goddess of ersatz pussies.

I rush to my girlfriend's house and proudly exhibit Fleshlight on her kitchen table. "Yup," she agrees. "Looks like a flashlight." But when I unscrew the top, there's this bubblegum-pink, puffy sphere with what appears to be a coin slot. We poke at it with our fingers: Hmm. Feels wet, but doesn't really make your finger wet—like that "goo" stuff for kids that comes in a little plastic trash can, only substantially more "adult."

"What's that smell?" Girlfriend sniffs inquiringly through her mid-January Kleenex-buffed nose.

I breathe in deeply myself. "Vanilla?"

"Christ on a crutch!" she squeals. "You're not gonna put your dick in that thing?"

"Why not? You wanna watch?"

"Yuck. Do it at your house."

"I can't do it at my house. You're supposed to warm it up in the sink by pouring hot water over it. My roommates will find out."

"Why don't you warm it up with a glass of wine, then?" she snipes.

Poor girl. She used to go out with a travel writer who sent her postcards from exotic places like China, Morocco, and Brazil. Now she's dating a pervert who only goes places he can get to on his Huffy. I open the bottom of the Fleshlight to discover a hard plastic tube that runs down the center. I pull on it and it sort of sticks to the pink, sticky "flesh."

"What is that?" she mutters. "Vulva-on-a-stick?"

I look at the brochure. "The stick maintains the 'vulva's' shape."

She runs her fingers through her hair and squints at the ceiling, "How symbolic." The brochure also warns not to share one's Fleshlight with *anyone*. No problem. I'm not even sure I want to share it with myself.

Girlfriend leaves the kitchen and climbs into her loft bed. Her cute little ass cupped inside a pair of velour bikini panties causes my all natural flesh battery to erect an electric arc of love. Then I look at Fleshlight cupped in my hands. One look at its vanilla, gooey-pink, coin-slot eye and I'm soft again. I crawl into girlfriend's loft bed and spoon around her warm, velour hips that house her real pussy. She clenches my hands between her breasts. Ah. Better.

"What about your date?" she asks.

"I left her with the toaster."

Next morning, while Girlfriend's in the shower, I'm nursing a coffee at the kitchen table. The sun's first rays cast a pleasing light across most of the room, and Fleshlight, which stands tall and majestic on the table, casts a shadow like a sundial. Maybe I will do it tonight.

After work I feel indecisive. Instead of racing home to fuck the gooey-pink eye, I find myself at one of those bars with a million different beers. It's midway between my house and Girlfriend's. Three connoisseurs to my left are talking fruity bouquets. I flirt with the idea of admitting defeat. Somehow my groin is not amused by Fleshlight. Could be the vanilla, could be the slime, could be the coin-slot eye.

I order a Boddingtons and watch Bartender-Girl build it the way you build a Guinness. The head rises to the top of the glass, then shrinks as the golden liquid emerges underneath in beer's more drinkable transparent form. I mean, it's not like I'm afraid of Fleshlight, is it? When the head settles, she pours another shot from the tap, slices off my foamy head with a butter knife, and slides the beer in front of me. Looking down into my head of my beer, I see a coin-slot eye. I raise the glass to my lips and it smells somewhat vanilla, and when I set it down

I'm acutely aware that a thin slime remains on my upper lip. I admit: I'm afraid. And once I realize I'm afraid, over the next couple of days, Fleshlight looms larger than life. It's my mother's disapproval, my third-grade teacher's declaration that I'll never amount to anything, my ex's aunt from Borough Park asking me why I'm not Jewish. It even argues politics and tells me to fine-tune my career in a more adult manner.

It's not like I'd go out and buy *Juggs* magazine, but they published one of my stories, and my contributor's copy came in the mail. As you may have guessed, they're into gooey, big breasts. In fact, they're into lactating mothers. Like a good egomaniac, I'm checking for typos over my morning coffee. Girlfriend's in the shower and I'm sitting at the table with Fleshlight. Today is my day off—my so-called writing day. It dawns on me that today is . . . *the* day. I pack my notebook, *Juggs,* and Fleshlight lovingly in my backpack and crack the bathroom door to kiss Girlfriend good-bye. "You think you could put the toilet seat back down every once in a while?" she complains.

"Women," I mutter as I struggle with my bike down the steps of her building, hoping it doesn't snow before I get to my place.

At my desk I try polishing up a story from years ago, and I rummage through my mail, working up to the task at hand. After my last piece of mail, I realize the time is now. I peruse my copy of *Juggs.* Hmm. That "virgin" chick on page nine is kind of cute. My, what a pretty pussy. Hmm. I'm horny. I quote my yoga teacher: "Be aware of your pud throbbing in its methodical yearning way." I turn the page. Hmm. The lactating mother. Haven't considered it and I won't begin now. My god, the boobs on that black lady with the carnival mask are bigger than my beer-gut. I need a little more porn star, a little less freak show. Ah, now there's a wholesome lass washing her pickup truck in someplace like Montana. She's wet and soapy and smiling this huge shit-eating grin in every shot, rubbing her boobs against the windshield of the truck so the photographer can get a shot from inside the cab. Yoga breath turns into panting.

I reach into my backpack for Fleshlight and hastily unscrew the top. Christ. Why vanilla? I realize it would be better to run it under hot water, but the roommates are all sitting around out there. I flip back to the "virgin's" lovely hymen-clad flower. She's smiling this smile that says, "Hi, perv!" while holding her eighteen-year-old hooters out to the camera. "Getting a hard-on?" She giggles. "Go on, take it out. Whack off for me, baby." She's also muttering, "Pathetic creep," under her breath, but I concentrate on her saying, "Go a step further, Joey. Undo your belt, sweetie. Your jeans, sugar lump. Your briefs, thumper."

"Okay," I answer.

"That's better," she coos as I scoot my pants down below my knees. "Now get your toy and lube up. . . ."

It's not easy. I remove the bottom lid as well as the top in order to remove the hard plastic tube from inside the soft, saccharine "vulva." I'm afraid of ripping it—as if it were a hymen or something—but eventually I wrestle it free. I put Fleshlight on the desk with its unfortunate pink coin-slot eye staring at the ceiling like a bored patient at an ophthalmologist's office, and snap the lid open on the lubricant. I aim into the coin-slot eye and get most of it in, but when I lift Fleshlight off the desk, the lubricant empties out the back end. It startles me and the thing falls from my hand, bouncing off the edge of my desk, off my thigh, and rolls onto the floor about six inches past arm's reach. I rock my chair sideways. Damn. I stretch, stretch more . . .

Knock. Knock. Knock.

"Uh, yes?"

"Can I come in?" my roommate Stephanie asks.

"No!"

"Then can I borrow some milk?"

"Borrow whatever the fuck you want!"

"Well, thank fuckin' you!" She yells safely, stomping away.

Ice-cold fake pussy juice is dripping from the puddle on my desk onto my lap. My pecker, soft as a jellyfish at this point, is burrowing backward into my flesh as my teeth start to chatter. Gee. If Mom could see me now, wouldn't she be proud?

I'm in serious need of a game plan. I rock my chair back and forth until I'm close enough to reach Fleshlight. Both of my hands are slick with lube but I manage to pull it onto my lap, where I "squeegie" some lubricant from the puddle between my legs back into the coin-slot eye. I wipe my left hand on my shirt and put the bottom back on before too much more can drip out.

I breathe deeply in that calming yoga way and casually flip through the pages of *Juggs,* trying to pretend that it's a warm, sunny Saturday and not forty degrees in my room. Now concentrate on the girl washing her truck in Montana. Nice. Cute butt—*and* butthole, I see. A very nice pink eye. Mmm, boobs. My trusty lust is taking over. I pick up *the thing.* I tip it over my dick. I slide it over the head. It's tacky. Kinda like a chick who isn't quite wet. My dick kind of bends cuz I'm only like 80 percent hard. To remedy the situation, I let go a warm string of steamy saliva onto my shaft. Shoulda done that instead of leaking that freezing lubricant all over the place. I turn back to the virgin cutie on page nine. There's a red line on her shoulder that her bra strap has left. "Babe," I tell her, "you're cute!" A couple of insurance pumps with my trusty right hand and, yes! Solid as a friggin' rock!

I re-enter like a bat into hell. There's a sensation down there of making it through the Sacred Gates of Labia. There's a Brazilian chick on page sixty-four with a deep, golden tan. She's so plump. So nice and plump. Like rotisserie chicken. She looks like what the Fleshlight feels like. Oh, yeah: Looks like what the Fleshlight feels like. She's squeezing her nipples in her fingers. The heels of her palms are plunging into her tit flesh. Wow! I'm getting it. It's gliding smoothly over my shaft while the Brazilian is graciously opening her pussy with her fastidiously manicured fingers in the next frame down. I plunge the thing over my dick to the hilt. Oh, yeah! Let the games begin! *Pfft. Pfft. Pfft.* Hey, it . . . the thing is hissing. I loosen the rear cap and plunge again. *PFFT! PFFT! PFFT!* It's hissing even louder. I take off the end completely, whether or not the fake pussy juice drips on my pants that are now bunched around the heels of my boots. The rotisserie Brazilian is so soft and plump, it's gonna be an easy ride home from here. I'm admiring her lovely full lips when it occurs to me that this thing feels like getting a blow job—only no teeth.

But sexy as the Brazilian is, I need Virgin Cutie from page nine to finish. I'm flipping back to her spread, pumping like a deranged plumber. There she is: holding her breasts up to her mouth, licking her nubile nipple. I'm pounding the squish out of the thing till it's bouncing off my nuts. Virgin Cutie is smiling, showing off the underside of her tongue while she licks her upper lip, showing off her labia, sphincter, and juggs. I get it! Finally, after years of writing this stuff, I get the whole pornography thing. See, anyone can do this. You don't gotta be a stud, you don't gotta be rich. You can be any fuck-up in the goddamn universe, alone in your room and horny, pounding the bejeezus away at something that won't scold you for leaving the toilet seat up. For just a moment, I'm lost in a sensation of bouncy, wet, somewhat virgin flesh, and boom! As Woody Allen would say, there's no such thing as the wrong kind of orgasm. Even the worst ones are right on the money.

Then it's over. I'm cold. The thing is dripping everywhere . . . and I have the urge to cuddle. The thing is quite unappealing right about now. I think about my sweetheart with her mid-January nasal drip, blowing her nose, but warm and huggable under a half dozen duvets. Virgin Cutie is still smiling the exact same smile from her frozen home on page nine.

"Hey, Joe!" Stephanie yells from outside my door. "Want anything from the fucking store?"

"Nah," I wheeze absentmindedly. "Just a hot shower."

WENDY BECKER
Backstage Boys

Tom B. is my stage name. It's short for "Tomboy," which is how everyone has referred to me since I was old enough to shock the housewives on my block by delivering their morning papers sporting only shorts, sneakers, and an assortment of Band-Aids.

Standing backstage, I watched Ernie Tulips perform, studying how his hips rocked slightly as he belted out his signature swing dance tune. He was one of the best drag kings in the Midwest, and as impatient as I was to perform, I was relieved not to have to follow his act.

There were two numbers left before mine, which meant I had about fifteen minutes to kill. I hated being ready early. I never knew what to do with myself while I waited.

Ernie moved into the dance portion of his number and I

imitated his smooth moves, trying to make them my own. It felt awkward. He was a crooner, k.d. lang meets Tony Bennett. I was Melissa Etheridge and Bruce Springsteen's love child, and Ernie's moves didn't match my jeans and white T-shirt. Still, there was nothing else to do. Step, cross, step-step-step . . . I was getting the hang of it . . . step, cross . . . I felt a hand on my ass.

Probably another drunk fag confusing me with Rob, one of the bartenders. Rob and I are about the same height and build, and we both have short black hair. Unless they were coming at us from the front, in a well-lit room, people regularly confused us, although as far as I knew, none of my buddies ever accidentally grabbed his ass. I couldn't say the same for his friends, whose greeting of choice seemed to be a five-fingered inspection of the right buttock. I turned around.

"Hey . . ."

"Keep your hands to yourself?" a fat butch woman suggested playfully. I hate being goosed, but I like women with big grins. "Danny," she said, extending her hand. She smelled like Ivory soap and leather.

"Tam, but I go by 'Tom B.' for the show. It's short for 'Tomboy.' What about you?"

"Just Danny," she replied, looking me up and down. I could feel her body heat.

"Oh." I'm so eloquent under pressure.

I heard applause and turned to see Ernie leave the stage. The emcee announced Ricky Rick, and a Latin beat started up.

Pretending to glance around, I snuck another look at Danny. Thirty-something, about 250 pounds, a little taller than me, probably five-foot-seven. Blond buzz-cut, sea green eyes, worn leather pants, and a long-sleeved black T-shirt. Leather pants and green eyes were two of my favorite things, though I typically liked the pants on myself and the eyes on a sultry femme with long, wavy hair.

I turned away before Danny could catch me looking at her. I didn't want to give her the wrong idea. As a general rule, I don't go for other butch women. It's not like I haven't slept with a few of my butch buddies, but it's always been equal parts wrestling and orgasm, the kind of sex where you have to flip a coin to see who lies back and takes it first.

"He's really good, but I bet you're better," Danny said, her voice low and close.

My heart started to beat faster. The crowd, and Danny, joined Ricky in the chorus. My temperature rose. The performance must have been affecting me. An arm wrapped around my torso, pulling me back into a warm, plaint body.

"You're irresistible, Tomboy," Danny whispered into my ear.

My heart skipped a beat. I wasn't used to being on the receiving end of butch pickup lines. She was smooth. Was I that smooth?

On stage, Ricky took off his jacket, then slowly unbuttoned his white shirt to loud catcalls and whistles. Danny's mouth brushed my neck, spreading goose bumps across my back. Her lips were as soft and gentle as those of the femmes I usually dated, but her arm kept me firmly pinned to her chest. I felt light-headed, so I leaned into her, glad for her size and strength. Her free hand found its way to my stomach, where it rested as she nibbled my ear. I was wet. So this is what the other side of seduction felt like.

"I'm going to take you, Tomboy," she said quietly.

Heat rushed through me. My legs felt weak and my clit was aching. I was suddenly drenched in sweat.

"If you don't want it, just step away now and we'll forget it," she continued.

I stayed put, rooted to the spot by my throbbing cunt. My ragged breathing prevented me from speaking. Her hand moved down to where my jeans met damp skin. I closed my eyes. Fingers entered the gap in my boxers. The Latin beat was replaced by a synthesized throbbing.

"Spread your legs," she commanded.

I complied willingly. She opened my labia and entered me slightly. I pushed onto her fingers.

Her strong, fleshy arm continued to grip me tightly as she bit my neck, hard.

"I'm marking you, Tomboy. You're mine tonight." I shivered involuntarily.

She pulled her fingers from my cunt and circled my clit slowly, her fingertips barely brushing me.

"Harder—please—more," I begged softly.

I was rewarded.

A moan escaped my lips, and her touch got feather-light again. Just when I thought I could take it no longer, she stroked me hard.

"Come for me," she ordered.

I hadn't realized it, but I'd been waiting for her permission. The release was sudden. It was all I could do to remain upright as I shuddered against her chest. When I was done, she turned me around and enveloped me in a hug. I sank into her arms, my scent mingling with her soap and leather.

"Sorry you missed your act," she said.

My act! Damn! I missed my cue. I guess fifteen minutes wasn't so long after all.

JERRY STAHL
From *Perv—A Love Story*

I didn't officially see her go. I made myself look away, pretending to watch for pedestrians. But I heard her, the first quick *wisssh,* then the sputtering gush. I saw the pee run and puddle the damp cement. A frothsy stream ran under my work boots but I didn't move. It wasn't piss. It was *her* piss.

I couldn't believe it. After my whole life, Michele's pussy was right there . . . *and I stared somewhere else.* When the puddling stopped, she tugged my pant leg. She raised her face and gave me a funny smile. "You want to?" Her voice was sweet and girlish again.

"Want to what?"

"You know, . . ." Shy and defiant at the same time. "Wipe me. Girls have to wipe when they pee, you know. My daddy always wiped me."

79

"Your daddy?"

Maybe I could tell her about Mom's cuddle-fish.

My mouth went so dry I could have spit wood chips. The sun peeped out of the clouds and everything looked super clear. More real than real. The wet crease between her legs was the color of champagne. My parents served it every New Year. I never liked the taste, but now sneaking a peek—because it was too much, because I would die or go blind—now I guessed I'd love it.

"I don't have any tissue," I sputtered, but Michele only shrugged.

"So?"

That's how it happened: in the middle of the Miracle Mile parking lot, I not only got to feel like I loved a girl, I got to feel when you touch one—down there—and love her at the same time. I trailed my finger so lightly on her slit, I hardly touched her at all. I'd have strangled puppies to do more, but there were all those people, those cars. All that light and traffic. The air felt like cold tinfoil.

I thought, idiotically, *What would Bob Dylan do?* Then I freaked. I imagined a station wagon owner footsteps away, ready to catch me. But catch me what? All I was doing—and I couldn't believe I was doing it—was brushing my hand along Michele's cleft, feeling the hot wet of her. The warm droplets in her champagne slit mingled with the chilly rain still on my fingers.

"Lick it," she said. Just like that. Matter-of-fact. "Lick it."

And, still standing over her, sort of leaning in, I slowly brought my hand up to my mouth. Yes! All the traffic noise seemed to fade away. The volume of the world had been turned down, leaving nothing but the roar of blood rushing from my balls to my ears. I let her see what I was doing. My tongue sponged along my knuckles, over the backs of my hands. I tasted the briny flavor of what I guessed was pee. I made a show of it, darting my tongue between my fingers, wiggling it, like a goldfish plucked out of its bowl. Then she spoke up again.

"I didn't mean that, Bobby. I meant this."

I stopped my knuckle lapping, looked down again, to where her finger was describing little circles. Her wrist blocked all but the purple-pink clit. "You know," she said huskily, "the little man in the boat."

"You mean . . . right here?"

My face got hot. I imagined police. Choppers swooping out of the sky, fixing us in a telephoto lens, filming everything, and presenting the evidence to a horrified jury. I could see the witnesses: Dolores Fish and Dr. Mushnik, Ned Friendly, Weiner, Tennie Toad and Farwell, and Headmaster Bunton. All of them dying to testify, itching to send me to Perv Jail.

My head wouldn't stop. I saw my mother, pill-drunk and burbling baby country-and-western, hiking up her salmon nightie and telling the judge, *"He wuvs to cuddle. . . ."* They'd drag her from the courtroom facedown in a box of turtles, yelping for electroshock. Somewhere in sweaty heaven, watching all of it, Mr. Schmidlap would crack a Rheingold with his flipper while Dad banged his head off the nearest wall.

"BOBBY!" Michele's harsh whisper brought me blinking back. "Bobby, *GO AHEAD*. Bobby, I *WANT* you to. . . ."

She touched herself and I shivered.

"But there's . . . I mean . . . There's all these people."

"I know," she said, but huskily, edging her back against the tire well of the VW bus. She parted her naked thighs slightly farther. "I know."

The way she studied me, it's like she was measuring some-

thing, seeing how far I'd go. Or else—and this really made my
stomach sink—how much I loved her. I was so hard I thought
my dick would crack off. But all those *people!* Those *cars!* The
weather . . .

You didn't think of sex and weather in the same breath. You
didn't have to. Not normally. Not ever. Except for here, in the
Miracle Mile parking lot, where Lela the Hare Krishna, who
used to be Michele Burnelka, was on the run from Shiva—
whoever Shiva was—and on her haunches for me. Whoever I
was. That's what I wrestled with. Not can I do this? But what
the fuck was it I thought I was doing? And who the fuck was
doing it?

Even the raindrops seemed to mock me.

"Michele," I stammered. I was ready, but then . . . A Negro
lady gawked at me from a Dodge Dart and it seized me up. I
had to pull the words like olives out of my throat. "Michele, I
can't . . . *I can't do it.*"

I heard myself and I died. It killed me to find out this was
me. I had everything I ever wanted. *AND LOOK WHAT
CAME OUT OF MY MOUTH!*

It wasn't like I was being a "good boy." It was like, I don't
know, like I was *scared.* Or not even scared, just . . . guilty.
That was it. My psyche sputtered like defective neon. One
thought wrenched my brain: Mom's seen a husband stroll under a streetcar. She's seen a daughter disappear to Canada, her
son fucked-up and flown home, kicked out of a pricey prep
school. If that weren't enough, picture her expression when I
was arrested for public pee tasting, or whatever the legal term
happened to be. How could I face her if I got popped for a sex
crime? For the ten zillionth time I wished I were an orphan,
like my long-gone father, just so I could relax.

Just to make things perfect, my voice squeeched into Jiminy

Cricket. "Michele, I really like you . . . I mean, I've always, like, loved you, it's just that . . ."

"Forget it," she said, her face hardening. She pulled up her pants and launched herself off the station wagon in a single movement, as though she'd been bouncing off cars and asphalt her entire life. "Forget it, Bobby. It's nothing."

"Really?"

This was so hugely untrue, so clearly not nothing, I hated myself for needing to hear it.

I held my hand out to help, but Michele ignored it and dusted herself off.

"You don't," she said with a brittle laugh, "you don't think I was serious, do you? You don't think I'm some kind of *exhibitionist.*"

"Gee, I don't know," I said. I just knew I wanted to rip my tongue out at the sound of "gee." This was worse than Jiminy Cricket. My voicebox had been hijacked by Wally Cleaver. Because I *never* said "gee." Never before and never since. I was not a "gee"-type person. But I couldn't tell Michele that. What was the point?

To Michele, from here on in, I'd be the geek who said "gee" and didn't have the balls to lick her pussy in broad daylight. With one move—or lack of one—I'd killed something horribly important. Whatever else happened, I knew I'd spend the rest of whatever time I had left walking upright, trying to redeem myself.

When Michele slouched off toward the highway, I resolved to be a bad-ass. A rebel. A daredevil. Keith Richards with Jewhair. Whatever it took to de-lame myself, that's what I'd do.

With no plan to speak of, I announced, "We need sleeping bags." To which Michele replied, "Sleeping bags cost money."

Remembering that she had all the money, and knowing I'd

look like an even bigger lightweight if I asked for it back—
suppose she said, "No!" Suppose she said, *"Fuck you!"* Then
what?—I heard myself mumbling, Marlon Brando–style,
"Don't worry about it. One thing I know how to do is steal."

And without another word, I headed back to the mall. Before I left, I thought I caught a flicker of respect in her eyes. It
gave me hope. (And a partial erection.)

I was back in ten minutes with a pair of lightweight goose-
downs, army green and waterproof.

When I handed hers over, I could tell she was impressed.
With any luck, I wouldn't have to knock off a gas station to
make her forget my cowardice. I could probably kill a man
with my bare hands and it wouldn't matter now. *Too-chicken-
to-lick.* It might as well have been tattooed on my forehead.
What do you do when you're branded and you know you're a
man?

Michele's eyes grew huge under her Beatles cap. At some
point, she'd dumped the rose-petal grannies, and I didn't miss
them. She squeezed the sleeping bag, then smiled. "You . . .
you stole these?"

"No big thing." I shrugged, and pretty much stood still
while she hugged me. I didn't want to look too eager. Didn't
want her to know what I felt. Most of all, I didn't want her to
accidentally touch my ass. The credit card was in my back
pocket. The last thing I needed was her finding out I charged
the bags to my mother.

DANI SHAPIRO
Bed of Leaves

Later, she will remember the leaves. The way they scratch and crumble against her back. The way her panties are smudged with dirt and she will have to ball them up and stuff them into her knapsack where her mother won't find them. Years later, as a woman, there will be a moment at the end of each summer when the scent of fresh-mowed grass will fill her lungs through an open car window, and she will close her eyes and her tongue will go soft, her inner thighs moist like the pale insides of a half-baked cake.

Eddie Fish is unbuttoning her shirt. There have been boys before this moment, boys who have stuck their fingers between her blouse and jeans, tugging the fabric loose, pushing their hands up around her bra and cupping her breasts. There have been boys—two, to be exact—who have unzipped her pants in the school basement, pushing their hardness against her cotton panties, eyes squeezed shut. But Eddie Fish is not a boy. Eddie is a man—twenty-eight years old—and Jennie knows these woods are about to become a part of her history. She is writing the story of her life, the story of her body on these damp suburban grounds with the man she has chosen precisely because he is a man.

The blond hairs on his wrists glisten as he reaches around her and unhooks her bra. She is impressed by his skill at bra unhooking, the ease with which he pulls the straps off her arms and hangs it on a nearby branch, a white cotton 32B flag of surrender. She is impressed by his warm dry palms that brush against her nipples, and by his eyes, dark blue in the noon of this clear Indian summer day, staring straight at her.

"Lisa Wallach," he says, murmuring the name of his last girlfriend as he stares at Jennie's breasts.

She looks at him, flushed.

"Sorry," he laughs, "I can't explain it. Your hair, your tits—you look just like her now—"

She doesn't know enough to be horrified. To slap Eddie Fish across his pale stubbled cheek, grab her bra off the branch and streak through the woods, away from him. Instead, she is flattered by the comparison to Lisa Wallach, who is a woman after all—at least twenty-six—and who is very beautiful in that frosted blond urban way. Lisa is a lawyer. She has an apartment in the city, and wears leather boots with stacked heels, long velvet skirts almost brushing the floor.

"What am I doing here with you?" he murmurs as he un-does the top button of her tennis shorts, bends down and un-laces each sneaker, pulls off her Fred Perry socks, small green abandoned wreaths. He unzips her shorts and shimmies them down around her ankles, along with her panties. Parts of her have never felt the breeze before. Her ass, her crotch, each nipple, seem to braid together into a rope twisting deep into her stomach, twining around itself, a noose that will remain forever inside her.

"Jailbait," he says, kissing her belly button.

Years from now, Eddie Fish will be a gynecologist in Scarsdale. He will drive a Volvo, own an espresso maker, be the father of two daughters of his own—two daughters he would kill if he ever found them in the woods with a man resembling his younger self.

But today, as he lights a joint and places it in Jennie's mouth, he is not focused on his future, the bright golden-boy future that unfurls before him like an heirloom rug. He has no doubts, no fears. His medical school degree is at the framers, his internship in the city will begin in just a few weeks, and Lisa Wallach is finally a thing of the past. And here is Jennie, the beautiful neighborhood kid with the crush on him, Jennie, twelve years younger than he—sixteen, for chrissake—three years ago he had attended her Bat Mitzvah! His eyes travel over her shoulders, down her breasts, lower to the blond depths of her. A virgin? He doubted it. She had written him letters all through medical school, letters so steamy he and Lisa had read them to each other late at night.

He stubs out the joint on a tree trunk, next to a carved heart with no names, no initials inside it.

Gently, he lays her down on a bed of leaves, her head resting against the root of a tree. She crosses her legs, her arms, trying to cover herself. She has no idea how sexy she is. He quickly pulls his polo shirt over his head, undoes his own shorts and steps out of them. Then, in his sneakers and tight white briefs, he lowers himself on top of her, careful to prop himself on his elbows.

Later, after it is all over, a friend will ask him why, after all, he did it.

"She was so beautiful," Eddie will say. "So fucking beautiful."

⟡

Eddie's head is between her legs. His mouth is moist, chin dripping, and he looks up at her as he twirls his tongue around and around. With his fingers, he spreads her apart.

"Are you using anything?" he asks.

"Yes," she says. She wants him to think she's a woman of the world. A woman whose motto, like a Boy Scout's, is "Be prepared." Her heart pounds as he slides a finger into her. Can he tell that she's lying?

He kisses her on the lips and she tastes herself. She is anticipating something awful, vomitous, some reason why her mother lines up bottles of sweet-smelling potions on the bathroom sill. She is surprised. The taste is not unpleasant: oceanic, vaguely like seaweed. Something dredged from the depths.

She wonders what he tastes like, if she will ever know.

Eddie wriggles out of his underwear and moves up her body so that his *thing,* this thing that she has been waiting for, is swinging above her mouth like a heavy, hypnotic pendulum. The last one she saw was Steven McCarthy's, back in third grade, when she accidentally on purpose opened the bathroom door while he was standing over the toilet.

Tentatively, she opens her mouth, darts out her tongue, runs her lips over the shaft. She is expecting something rough, something that feels like stubble. She is surprised by his smoothness, and she lifts her head up and covers him, her hair falling over him as he moans a high-pitched sound she has never heard before, blending into the chirps and rustles all around them. Suddenly, Eddie pushes himself farther into her mouth with a small grunt and she tastes something faintly metallic at the back of her throat.

"Whew," he says, pulling away from her. "You sweet thing. Where'd you learn *that*?"

She feels heat rise from her breasts to her cheeks. Without even looking, she knows that a blotchy red rash has spread across her chest and neck, a map to her inner world. She always turns blotchy when she feels anything complicated. She fights back the urge to gag at the drop of thick slippery fluid trickling down her throat.

"I almost came," he said with a grin. "Naughty girl."

He slides down her body, his stomach pressed against her own, and thrusts into her. Jennie braces herself and grits her teeth, waiting for the pain. Will there be blood between her legs? Will he find out she's a virgin and recoil? Jennie knows this: Eddie Fish does not want her to be a virgin. For the rest of her life, boyfriends and husbands will ask about her first time, and the name Eddie Fish—that unfortunate moniker— will forever be whispered in a progression of beds.

Who was you first?

Eddie Fish.

And how was it, my darling?

It was—it was what it was.

He has pushed all the way inside her and she feels nothing. No pain, no magic. Her insides have widened to accommodate him as if a door has always been open, as if a room inside her has been drafty, just waiting to be entered.

Her breath seems loud to her ears, and her heart pounds erratically as Eddie moves to the rhythm of music only he can hear. She tries to time her heart, her breath, to his. *Ba-da-dum, ba-da-dum.* A tribal forest beat. The hairs on his thighs tickle her and she fights an urge to break into hysterical giggles. Her stomach is hot beneath him, an interior soup. She twists her head to the left and sees Eddie's hand flat against the dirt, his wrist encircled by a thin strand of leather that she remembers Lisa Wallach brought him from Brazil. The leather strand had magical powers, Lisa told him, and he would have very bad luck if he unknotted it himself. Jennie wonders if Eddie Fish will wear that strand of leather until it disintegrates.

Eddie speeds up. A vein in his throat pops out and he is looking down, down to the place where their bodies are joined. With a gasp and a grunt, he collapses on top of her. Jennie can feel his heart through her chest. Eddie Fish's heart! She will remember this moment, she promises herself: the faded blue summer sky, the worm inching along the edge of a pale yellow leaf, the soft smell of dirt. She will color it with a patina of great beauty. She thinks about Eddie's question—*Are you using anything?*—and her fingers grow icy. She wonders if it can happen the first time, if the grassy mess oozing between their legs can grow into something more complicated—a punishment, a life sentence. She closes her eyes and prays: *Just this once, never again, please not now,* a jumble of wishes.

"What?" asks Eddie, looking down at her.

"Sorry?"

"Your lips were moving."

"Oh, it's nothing."

"You're not getting weird on me, Jen, are you?"

She doesn't answer. *Getting weird.* Eddie's words echo and bounce through her skull. She twists her neck once again, her cheek resting on the cool earth, and stares at the empty heart carved into the base of the tree. She imagines her own initial there and then, like a stack of cards flipping through the wind, a hallucination, she sees the initials of every man who will ever become her lover. There are so many—perhaps dozens! More than she can possibly imagine. She is filled with the knowledge of what she does not know.

Eddie kisses her throat, his lips dry and papery, then jumps up and rummages for his briefs beneath a pile of fallen leaves. He looks down at Jennie and she squints at him, blinded by the sunlight behind his shoulder. From where she lies, he seems like a giant.

"I—I didn't use anything, Eddie," she falters.

He stumbles on one leg, awkward as he pulls on his underpants.

"What did you say?" he asks, stopping.

"I'm sorry—I didn't use anything," she says, this time with greater conviction.

"Jesus, Jennie!" He punches the air. "How could you—"

"I didn't know."

"But I thought you were—"

Tears stream down her face. The light, the woods, are refracted, kaleidoscopic. Eddie Fish's face becomes a blur.

"You bitch!" she hears, as if from a great distance. He is walking away from her, heels crunching against the leaves. "If anything happens, it's not my problem, do you hear me?"

Slowly, she gathers her things. She pulls her bra from the branch, stuffs her panties into her knapsack, buttons her blouse and yanks on her shorts. She sits back down against the tree and searches the ground for a sharp twig. When she finds it, she begins scratching her initials into the empty heart, digging deep into the bark. She works carefully, with the precision of an artist. She fills the whole perimeter, so there will be no room for anyone else.

DODIE BELLAMY
Spew Forth

Desperate times call for desperate measures. I was eating goat-milk ice cream at Veggie Kingdom when I first saw Anya. It was 1979. A petite woman in her early thirties walked from table to table smiling demurely—shoulder-length blond hair cascaded in soft waves about a pretty, perky face with an upturned nose—she looked like a cross between Michelle Pfeiffer and Lady of *Lady and the Tramp*. "That's Anya," someone said. The most incredible dress floated about her slight frame, layer upon irregular layer of pale blue chiffon, perforated throughout with holes, biggish ones, as if someone or something had once been trapped inside and punched its way out. "That's Anya Steppes," continued the man at the next table. "I love her dress," I said. "It's a replica of the native costume of Venus." "Venus?" I blurted out. He leaned over his soy-grit stroganoff. "Yes, Venus—for Anya's a walk-in."

"What's a walk-in? Is that somebody who comes in without a reservation?" He smiled at me with his dark smudged hair, his graphite eyes, infinitely patient. He had an unusually high forehead, like *Eraserhead,* but cute. My hand reached toward him through the bright vegetarian air, and our pointer fingers touched with a spark like the fingers of those burly naked gods in that famous, who did it, da Vinci, Michelangelo? "Hi, I'm Carla, Carla Moran." "Yes." He nodded knowingly. "I'm Steven. A walk-in is an enlightened soul who returns to Earth by taking over the body of a lesser soul who no longer wishes to inhabit it. The enlightened soul meets with the unhappy soul on the astral plane and says, 'Hey, I can help you out.' And so the body survives a suicide or a violent accident, then reawakens with the walk-in soul who works to raise the consciousness of mankind. Lots of geniuses and humanitarians through the years were walk-ins— Albert Schweitzer, Benjamin Franklin, Beethoven, the guy who invented the atom bomb. Anya took over the body of a twelve-year-old girl—from Tennessee—who died in a car wreck."

I swallowed the last spoonful of goat-milk ice cream, it had a gamy afterbite like buckwheat or deer, but you got used to it. "Wow!" "Anya's an advanced soul—*very* advanced—here to bring the ancient spiritual teaching of Venus to Earth—she's written a book about it, *One Touch of Venus.*"

Later I would sleep with Steven, later I would hear of Anya dancing on a table in a leopardskin bodysuit, cleavage Venusians never dreamed of, later I would hear how she fucked like a big blond cat, clawing and screeching *From Venus she came*— but that first time in Veggie Kingdom I was so starstuck I dropped my water glass—CRASH—Anya turned toward me and her blue dress twirled with her, thin and translucent as dragonfly wings.

Steven put me on the mailing list of *The Venusian Tattler,* a newsletter that would keep me abreast of Anya's radio and TV appearances. "If astronauts landed on Venus," Anya'd tell her avid or skeptical host, "it would appear empty—save to the most enlightened—because Venus exists on a higher vibratory rate than here on Earth. We, the creative, evolved inhabitants of Venus all have blue eyes and blond hair. Life on Venus is more permeable than on your planet—that's why this dress I'm wearing is full of holes." I learned from Anya that life "on the physical" is but a phase, and therefore thoughts are actions—and that Jesus Christ was a lower initiate who diluted the Venusian teachings to match the (lower) consciousness of his era. On Venus, people could walk through trees or visit shimmering temples filled with all the great books that ever have been or ever will be written. Venusians didn't need to read these books—through osmotic transference their higher selves were directly linked to the wisdom of the universe.

I placed a copy of *One Touch of Venus* under my pillow—in my little flat on Valparaiso Street in San Francisco's North Beach—so that while I slept its secret teachings would drift into my etheric body, and I would understand with a depth that I never before dreamed possible. The inner Anya knew this, knew that I was tuned in to the higher vibrations of her late night talk-radio chatter, knew that I was ready to take the next step. The following Thursday night, Friday morning, really, I wrapped myself in my pink chenille bathrobe and switched on my "portable" Zenith radio, black and chrome it was, mono, built like a tank. Anya flirted with the deejay as usual. I propped a pillow against the wall, leaned back in my bed, and lit a cigarette, comforted by her high bell-like giggles. "You're some far-

out chick," the deejay punned. "Rapping with you's like taking
a hit of acid with a sinsemilla chaser!" Anya's voice deepened,
thickened like stormclouds. "Drugs and cigarettes burn holes in
your aura," she declared. "Holes where demons burrow!" I was
smoking two packs of Merits a day and lots of grass, and then
there were those mushrooms my roommate brought back from
Mexico, and the blotter acid I dropped before the Sarah Vaughn
concert and the MDA I took by mistake . . . my poor astral body!
Punctured and ravaged as a slab of charred Swiss cheese! I felt
light-headed, lightened by decay, invisible claws caressed my
throat, invisible lips whispered sinful seductions. I grabbed the
radio for support, its antenna quivered in the chilly, deathly still
air. "Before you know it," continued Anya, "you're a nympho-
maniac food-junkie alcoholic druggie, feeding the ravenous desires that keep demons clinging to our planet." Oh no! I took
one last drag and threw my cigarette out the window. It spun
like a falling star to the playground below.

I pulled *One Touch of Venus* out from under my pillow and
looked up "demons" in the index. There was a column and a
half of entries! **Demons, auras:** Demons wear binoculars
around their necks to spot new holes in your aura, will use
every trick in the book *money flesh cares of this world persecution*
to get their fix. **Demons, interruptions:** They drizzle sand on
your head as you read inspirational texts, tickle the feet of babies to make them scream during spiritual lectures **WAAAH!**
Straight to hell you'll go on an elevator, a demon's blazing finger pushing the buttons. **Demons, language:** The vilest grunts
vomit from their mouths, snarls too obscene to be translated
into English—imagine construction workers' mouths raised
to the highest power—every word in the demon's lexicon is
obscene, as is their grammar, their punctuation, their dingbats,
their typography, which is now *your* druggic lexicon *your* ciga-

rette grammar *your* punctuation *your* dingbats. Every excla-
mation point is a rape-fuck!!!!!! Demon-sprache is blotched
with underlines italics outline roman bold, putrid indecipher-
able swirls and stars—demons slap their foreheads, bug or
scrunch their eyes, point to their temples and stick out their
tongues; excretions bubble forth. *MAN OH MAN* @#!!!**
HEY **WOW!** Pod-shaped bodies, waddling blobs of emo-
tional cacophony, **"AWK!"** when the Devil chastises one, he
clenches the edge of a paragraph, hands and feet poking into
the margin, toes crimped under like odious question marks,
halo of sweat, jack-o'-lantern mouth ripped open, "GULP
OHHH **NOOO** *AIEEEEE!"* Arms scrawny and naked as
plucked chickens.

I flushed my cigarettes, grass and diet pills down the toilet
and went after Steven like a steamroller. Steven ran the
Golden Gate Venusian Study Group, which met every
Wednesday evening in the basement of Noe Valley Ministry.
A thousand-holed white ceiling, fluorescent lights gleaming
across the speckled linoleum floor, dark fiberboard paneling,
dehumidifier humming in the corner, a handful of seekers sitting in folding chairs in a circle, eyes closed, chanting the secret Venusian mantra:

OOOOHH-HOOOOOO-AAIIIIIIIIIIII-EEEEEEEE-
AAAHHHNNNNNNNN-YYYAAAAAAAHHHH-
OOOOHH-HOOOOOO-AAIIIIIIIIIIII-EEEEEEEE-AA
AHHHNNNNNNNN-YYYAAAAAAAHHHH-
OOOOHH-HOOOOOO-AAIIIIIIIIIIII-EEEEEEEE-
AAAHHHNNNNNNNN.

When we opened our eyes the room looked slightly
blurred—brighter, lighter, the air effervescent with spiritual
energy. Steven was high-vibed and businesslike, never gave
me the time of day. He seemed to favor this other woman,

Marsha—Marsha, who was always acting so syrupy holy in her puff-sleeved dresses, well, I could see right through that holiness of hers, it had more holes in it than the ceiling. Desperate times call for desperate measures—one Wednesday evening I showed up in my seduction outfit: low-slung bell-bottoms that barely covered the crack of my ass and my soft, fuzzy baby blue cardigan. It was tight enough to gape open, with a plunging V-neck. No bra. When I wore this sweater to the food stamp place, the guy gave me a month's worth without even asking to see my ID. I lingered after the meeting as Steven put away the folding chairs, his hair was still darkly smudged, his eyes still graphite. Large, clumsy hands I found endearing. "Carla, can I help you?" he asked. "Yes," I said, batting my Maybelline eyes. "Steven, it's just that there are certain aspects of the Venusian educational system"—dramatic pause, heavy eye contact—"that I just can't grasp." And so it began. His cock was large and his fucking was relentless and cold, it hurt like hell *not HELL!!!* I closed my eyes and imagined I was dying in a blazing plane crash and Steven's cock was a walk-in breaking through the physical barrier. His cum would fill me with glory and enlightenment.

Steven was a Viet Nam vet, which I found *way* romantic, all that intensity. He drove for City Cab, but his dream vocation was to sketch tourists' portraits at Fisherman's Wharf. He already had a much-coveted street vendor's license. Once when we were brunching at Zims he drew me on a napkin, a jagged cartoon woman with vertical slashes for hair. "But it doesn't look like me." Steven's heavy brows furrowed, he reached across his eggs Benedict, took my hand: "It's your inner self." Steven eventually gave up representation—he didn't want to be tied to the physical—and began painting bright biomorphic masses that floated around one another like jigsaw pieces suspended in Jell-O. Depending upon their colors, they were called "Life," "Soul," "Etheric," or "Serenity." He also made mobiles, the same blobby shapes cut from cardboard boxes, painted with Day-Glo acrylic and hung from twisted coat hangers—the air flowing between the forms, he said, was Spirit directing their movements. For our second date he picked me up at five A.M. in his cab and we drove to the Bay to watch the sun rise. Steven shuddered, remembering the rats in Viet Nam, rats as big as cats *we were souls inhabiting human bodies, we told each other, with enough spiritual discipline we could break the bonds of this plane, visit the wisdom temples, the white deserts of Venus* my heart, like the horizon, turned golden, pink, extravagant.

I had a master's degree, but I was still a child, I'd had sex maybe twenty times with fifteen men, but never a boyfriend. When, after a couple of months, Steven announced he no longer wanted to fuck me, I started crying. I'd always been willing, I even kind of liked it *why why why why why why* . . . "Steven," I pleaded, "what did I do wrong?" "Nothing, Carla, you did nothing, it's just that after Anya, Earth women just don't do it for me, or not for long, that's all." Anya, Anya, Anya! Long ago she'd moved to Berlin, Anya didn't even send him postcards anymore but he would never move on to me, how bland I must seem how *nothing* beside Anya's Venusian tantra, her extraterrestrial tricks. I sniveled, my lower lip trembling like the San Andreas fault. He pulled a hanky from his pocket and handed it to me, it was large and white and so soft. "Steven!" I wailed. "Don't worry," he said, taking me in his arms, "there's no reason we still can't sleep together, we just won't fuck, and I'll wear my Jockeys." And that's just what we did, sort of. I hated those Jockeys, standing between me and his creamy flesh *vile cotton* like Tristan and Isolde's sword. I continued to sleep naked, to spite them. Steven would wait for a perfect moment of unwillingness, when I was asleep or pissed off—the jockeys would vanish and he'd crawl on top, force my legs apart and bang into me so hard my guts sloshed upward squishing my lungs BREATH as he climaxed he yelled out, "WHAT IS *HAPPENING* . . . TO ME!!!!" Then he rolled over and we never talked about it. Once I inadvertently came too. "That was great!" I exclaimed to his back. Steven turned around, his face skewed with disgust. "You treat me like I'm your stud."

Heterosexuality continues to this day to surprise me, the things men present to you as normal *I wondered what was wrong with me that Steven didn't want to fuck me* if a demon bites you teeth marks appear on inaccessible parts of your body, wounds you couldn't possibly have inflicted yourself *white-coated attendants rush in and strap your wrists to the bed, across your chart the shrink scrawls HYSTERIA* on my back, legs open . . . body-heat bearing down on me, a bellowing boiling cloud, steam tunneled into my cunt scorching clit and lungs, I spread wider *what heaven this brimstone* and moaned, "Steven your thrusts are out of this world." No answer. Then I remembered *Steven's at work and I'm alone in the bed or should be* a body I couldn't see was fucking the shit out of me *the thickness of touch* demon fingers palpated my breasts, indentations dappling across my chest like magic *sparse bristles on back, lines of energy rippling along calves and forearms, hairless armpits, no genitals, demon noses are long as dicks* blow dryers hidden beneath their nostrils crystallize the moisture in your cunt so that a nose rammed up there chafes and shreds the parched flesh OUCH! When a demon fucks you with its dildo-nose it comes with a big ACHOO *snot for semen* there isn't time for birth control *not a minute* still it took me a full six months to become pregnant.

For we wrestle not against flesh and blood, but against prin-
cipalities.

After the abortion I started going to a holistic therapist
named Donna, a cute woman with shiny brown shoulder-
length hair and a chipper smile. She was older than I but still
not very old. These are some of the things I never told her
about: Steven my fear of being locked in public restrooms
trapped alive Anya my terror of falling asleep of turtleneck
sweaters of pot lucks of salt shakers and sugar jars in restau-
rants of people on drugs of catching their highs and what if my
hands took on a will of their own. My elevator phobia: I would
arrive fifteen minutes early, trudge up the six flights to her office, dawdle in the hall until I quit panting. "You look so exotic
in those blue earrings," she'd coo. "What adventures has life
brought you this week?" "Oh nothing in particular." "*Nothing?*" Deeper and deeper did I hunch into the white wicker
armchair with its cheerful floral cushion, tainted and abject,
my lips a trembling wall of nondisclosure. My eyes traced the
arabesques of the Oriental rug on the floor. Donna stared at
me, her face pleasant and blank until I finally blurted out, "I
throw up." "Throw up?" "Yes." "I'm all ears," she chirped. I
babbled on about how I was vomiting at least twice a day and it
had been over a year—the weight loss was great, I felt intense
and sexy, like Joan Jett—but I read about all these women with
rotting teeth. She listened, therapeutically silent, then cocked
her head and said, "What sign are you?" "Aquarius." Her head
shot erect, shiny brown hair jiggling against the lace collar of
her blouse: "Yes." Some planet was imminently moving into
some house. "So you see," she chimed, "when you're ready to
give it up, your bulimia will drop away." We decided to focus
on something positive. Donna hypnotized me and we found a
safe spot on my thigh that I could touch whenever I felt afraid.

The following week she was unusually somber. Her green eyes raced up and down my body like a bar-code scanner, then she pointed a finger at me and intoned, "Demonic possession!" She grabbed the silver fairy ball that dangled from her neck on a velvet cord and began rubbing it quickly, the shiny silver ball rolled about between her pert little breasts reflecting the room, reflecting *me* like a third wide-angle eyeball, its tiny clapper tinkling erratically as if the fairy inside were having an epileptic attack. "Vomiting is your soul's way of telling you to get rid of something, only until now you hadn't figured out what." DEMONS!!!! I hadn't smoked cigarettes or done any drugs for nearly nine months, these holes in my astral body, would they ever heal? Silently I chanted, OOOOHH-HOOOOOO-AAIIIIIIIIIIII-EEEEEEEE-AAAHHHNNNNNNNNN-YYYAAAAAAAHHHH. "Have you," I queried timidly, "considered hysteria?" According to Donna, depression and possession go hand in hand—demons crowd your head, causing your brain to swell and press against the skull *like water-weight, like psychic PMS.* "Let's do a little spring cleaning!" I close my eyes and she tells me that my arm is weightless, that helium balloons are lifting it. When my outstretched arm floats in front of me she says, "Demons, can you hear me?" I nod. "Demons, when you died you should have passed quickly to the Other Side, but something went wrong and now you're lost between worlds. I'm here to help you find the way home." Behind my eyelids there is only mottled black, I squint and try to focus these confused beings, whom I imagine to be elongated and wavering. "If you look really hard, you should be able to see a light. Can you see it?" The demons nod. "You don't belong with Carla, you belong with your friends and family who are waiting for you in that light, let go of Carla's aura, walk towards the light. Are they walking?" I nod. "Say good-bye." My floating arm bobs up and down. "Have a nice afterlife, demons. Carla, when I count to ten, you'll be fully conscious and refreshed." But I hadn't seen anything, no lights, no demons, no nothing *I FAILED MY OWN EXOR-CISM* at home I ate a pint of Chocolate Fudge Swirl and threw it up. As I wiped the sweet acidic froth from my mouth I thought I heard someone or some*thing* mutter, *You're going to pay for your big fucking mouth,* but when I turned there was nothing, nothing but air.

That night Steven took me to the Royal to see *The Entity.* Invisible forces pummel a female torso, tiny craters dimple across the breasts, but it doesn't really look like human flesh, more like the impressions made by your finger when you poke a ball of yeast dough, soft hollows that of their own accord rise back up. But Barbara Hershey is great, so convincing as her body is rhythmically slammed against the bed the couch the wall **AIEEEE AWK!** Scientists trap the demon in a mountain of liquid nitrogen, but it breaks out. Afterward Steven said, "Want to go to Sweet Creations? My treat." "Sure!" As we crossed Polk Street he wrapped his arm around my waist, and I wriggled my hand into the back pocket of his Levi's. From a car radio Phil Collins crooned, "There's something in the air tonight." And he was right, something *was* in the air, a clarity, a heightened charge—I could feel it in the way the concrete sparkled beneath the streetlights, in the aurora borealis of water standing along the curb, in the way the sky sprawled upward and outward forever, a vivid midnight blue. Three-dimensionality seemed to be swelling and stretching like a huge wad of bubble gum, and when it popped a whole new realm would spew forth, a realm filled with harmony and love. The infrared heat of Steven's ass cupping my open palm. Minutes later I spotted the chubby cherubs that frolicked across Sweet Creations' window—damn!!!—I wasn't ready to break free of Steven's body, wanted to curl myself around him even tighter, like a serpent in Eden. We entered the tiny health-food bakery, ordered at the counter and took a window seat, the thick sweet scent of honey infusing our hair, our clothes, our words. Steven reached across the table and covered my hand with his large clumsy claw. His electric warmth zapped along my arm and into my cunt *ooohh* I gnawed my leaden sesame cookie and smiled and basked. His dark eyes seemed to glow with new light *intoxicating eyes* a world map spread across the wall behind him, the tip of South America pointing down like a fat finger to the top of his head. "Look, Steven, South America's pointing straight at your crown chakra!" We had a good chuckle over that one. "Barbara Hershey was amazing," I said. "She must have really been molested by demons." Steven sipped his ginseng tea and nodded in agreement. "If any Hollywood star was, it was Barbara Hershey!" He recalled her 1971 rebirth as Barbara Seagull. For one low-budget production she had to kill a seagull on film. It was so freaked out when it died, its spirit flew into her body. "So she took the name Seagull—Barbara Seagull. Like Anya, she's a walk-in! It ruined her career for years. And this movie *The Entity* is her comeback." I squeezed Steven's callused thumb. Maybe tonight was my night for a comeback too.

Steven lived in the Casa Mia, a tidy residence hotel on Columbus near Union. Dorm fridge beneath the sink in the corner, ten-speed leaning against the window, the snores of an old Italian filling the lightwell. As I sat on the edge of the bed taking my shoes off, Steven said, "You told didn't you, you told your therapist about me and you, you told her about the holes in your aura, the *demons* didn't you." I nodded guiltily *how did he know* Steven's high brow collapsed into wrinkles. "I gotta take a piss." I jumped up and grabbed his sleeve. "Wait, Steven, I told her *some* things, but not about you and me." "That's what you think." He shook me off and slammed the door. I went over to the sink for a glass of water, not that I was thirsty, but in the movies they're always offering distressed people water. "Your son's dead, here have a glass of water." As I lift the forest-green tumbler to my lips, I hear the sound of horse hooves pounding densely packed medieval earth, the rattling of windows, willow branches lashing against the panes. A crack opens up in the linoleum, then a golden face emerges with seven glowing green eyes arranged in the shape of a cross. I stoop down and push the middle one, it swirls and steams with molten blood and a pit opens at my feet that extends to the beginning of time and the Earth's hellish core. The colors in the room brighten, glow, swirl, then sag and drip, a glowing blankness. I step around the pit toward the bed, suddenly naked, staring straight into another world where mirrors register monkey heads, my toenails painted blood red. I float downward onto the mattress, gently, the mattress is cold and hard, a marble slab, no dialogue but a thousand fat white candles, their flames lapping the air. Steven enters wearing nothing but his 501s, biceps inflated, he paints ancient symbols on my midriff with a red brush, cold tickle, his face more angular—bestial—than usual as he mounts me, and then I see it his giant lizardy eye, I let out a little scream Oh! His carefully manicured claws, two inches long, luminescent green, brush my cheeks, his horns reach skyward, his long ears droop downward straight to hell, the vertical furrows in his brows *up and down up and down* his huge mouthful of teeth his acres of gums, lava red, gleaming with demon cum, it leaks out all his orifices whenever he's aroused *desperate times* he throws his head back, fucks me slowly and clumsily, his giant wings cumbersome, more jagged than angel wings *my cunt a gash between dimensions* his tail hangs down in the crack of his ass as he humps forward, the marble slab is so cold so hard *love is bruises love is bruises* I only see him in quick cuts, occluded by the sizzling haze of hell but he is truly a marvel to behold, his bubbly luminescent green hide, his sulfurous breath hot as a blowtorch on my flimsy cheeks, his molten red cock, two feet long with a spear-shaped head, there are words inside it, molten words *dreams unwind love's a state of mind* misty psychedelic colors undulate as he brays he loves me in Latin backwards. I am insatiable *my name is Legion* can't get enough of his demon cock *for many demons have dwelled within this body* ripped open by this snorting cloven creature *red face forked tongue* sweating and heaving I come quickly, a fireball of sulfurous farts explodes from my bloody loins, my screeches break the sound barrier, rattling the tranquil vibes of Venus, booming back I cry out, **YIKES! <u>AIGGEUUUU!!!!</u>**

DAN TAULAPAPA McMULLIN
Sunday

There was a seminary student from Samoa. His parents escorted him to Minnesota. He was the first Samoan Lutheran seminary student. There are Mormons, Catholics, Congregationalists, all over Samoa. But he was the first Lutheran. His parents stood on either side of him in the middle of Nicolett Mall on a summer day. In the same spot where Mary Tyler Moore threw her hat into the air.

The Reverend Knarffssen came out of his cathedral at the north end of the mall. Approaching the three Polynesians, he suddenly smiled. Winter was so far away. Somewhere among the gargoyles. "Such warm, happy people," was his first thought.

"I shall treat Pali as I treat my own son, the assistant reverend," the Reverend Knarffssen told Mr. And Mrs. Saolefaleoteinemauga, taking Pali's moist brown hand and touching it to his dry cheek.

Mr. and Mrs. Saolefaleoteinemauga beamed smiles like tropic birds floating slowly across their high faces: Mr. Saolefa-leoteinemauga staunch as the sides of Savaii and Mrs. Saolefa-leoteinemauga a single column of devotion and prayer. "Take care of our boy." Pali, six foot five, looked down at the five-foot-five Reverend.

"I will," said the Reverend, and lowered his head in a few words of thanksgiving while his eyes traced the ascending lines of Pali's thighs.

Summer in Minnesota was hot and green. Then, as happens annually in Minnesota during the third week of October, winter descended swiftly with snow and ice.

Christmas came and went. Pali was invited to spend part of winter break with the Reverend Knarffssen and his son Gregg, the assistant pastor. Pali wondered about the rumor that Gregg and the Reverend were not actually related by blood but by common interest, as he noted the difference in physical appearance during the first sauna the three of them took together.

In fact, the three of them were sitting naked in the Pastor's basement within fifteen minutes of Pali's arrival, coming into the house after the drive from the seminary in town with Gregg. The Pastor, bounding down the stairs in his bathrobe, invited Pali to join them for their afternoon invigorating Swedish sauna. Before you could say, *Uff da!*, Pali was on a high pine bench pouring spring water from a wooden dipper, watching eucalyptus-scented steam rise between him and his nude hosts. Pali wore a towel, having been brought up a modest Christian Samoan.

"I would have thought that being Polynesian," said the Pastor, plumbing his bottomless well of ignorance, "you wouldn't have hangups about nudity and such things."

"We were brought up never to swim on Sundays and always to wear a T-shirt to the beach," answered Pali.

"Oh, how we must have fucked you poor bastards up the ass," moaned the Pastor, standing on floor level and looking into the shadow under Pali's towel, thinking of missionaries.

Pali took a moment to ponder this. His embarrassment at the casual nudity forced him to keep his eyes above the Pastor's jawline, and he refused to acknowledge Pastor Knarffssen's erection. From the Pastor's pale, boyish body, with its slim hips and small ass, there curving upward toward his chest sat a great fat colorless prick that glistened around the head as precum dribbled onto the blond floor. "Actually most of the Christian missionaries to Samoa came from Rarotonga," was Pali's response.

The Pastor tweaked the head of his prick, making it pink, and coated the round shaft with a palm full of stuff. The smallness of the Pastor's torso made the long curve of his hard-on all the more incredible. But Pali's discretion was boundless. Even a stiff dick with a heartbeat, trembling between his ankles in the steam, would not alter his respectful attention to his mentor's words.

The Pastor sat down on the bench at Pali's feet with a sigh. "Gregg, why don't you do your exercises?" he suggested. Gregg was not immune to the charms of the Pastor's member—it was the Pastor's one physically alluring quality. But today, he felt shy around Pali. Rather than taking the Pastor's hidden cue, he began instead to actually exercise.

Gregg started with stretches. He sat on the high bench opposite Pali. Spreading his legs, he touched his fingers to the tips of his toes. The sauna was quiet with only the sound of

Gregg's breathing and the creaking bench—and Pastor Knarffssen's yanking. Gregg and the Pastor together glanced at the dark brown nipples on Pali's broad chest softening in the heat.

Pali looked curiously at Gregg. He was as tall as Pali and as broad shouldered. While the Pastor was narrow, Gregg had thick thighs and a jutting, dimpled ass, perfectly round. While the Pastor was covered in invisible white hairs that tickled anyone he sat by, Gregg was a smooth slab of corn-fed farm-boy. "They're not related at all," Pali decided.

"Oh, flex that ass," muttered the Pastor, watching his assistant.

"This reminds me of Fiji," said Pali.

"Why Fiji?" asked the Pastor.

"I used to go swimming with the Catholic seminarians there—this was before I decided to study the teachings of Martin Luther," said Pali.

"Where'd you swim?" asked the Pastor.

"At a waterfall near Suva. Once a Tongan woman from New Zealand joined us, she said she was a writer; we could see her breasts under her wet lavalava, and she said all sorts of suggestive things!"

"Like what?" asked the Pastor.

"I made hors d'oeuvres!" said Gregg, jumping up and running out of the sauna.

"My son is nervous today," said the Pastor. "You'd think it was the first time we've had a guest from overseas."

⑥

The snow was ripping through the air outside. Pali stood in the master bedroom wearing a lavalava that the Pastor had given him. "I've bought one for each of us! They're Polynesian pareos," said the Pastor.

"It looks Malaysian," Pali said, noting the paisley patterns.

"So it's true they don't wear anything underneath?" said the Pastor, rubbing his eyebrow, looking down at his tent.

"Suits the climate," said Pali. "I can't seem to find any of my clothes right now."

"Probably in the laundry," said the Pastor, "We always try to get the visitors' effects immediately into the wash. Seminarians!" The Pastor tried pressing his hard-on against Pali's hipbone.

Pali felt only *ava, faaaloalo,* and *alofa mo le toeaina:* respect, reverence, and love for one's elder. He found the Minnesota Lutheran clergyman's home life exotic. He went down the stairs and into the carpeted living room. The Pastor, chasing after him, tucked the hem of his pareo into the waistband, his now shrinking but still swollen member tossing up and about.

"Pali! Pali! I just want to chat!" shouted the Pastor as Pali dodged the oak furniture and scattered Pastor Knarffssen's extensive collection of wooden craft items. Knocking over an elmwood rabbit, Pali raced through the kitchen and out onto the sundeck. The snow was now flying about in big wet flakes, hitting Pali's black hair and smooth back. Like footballers in training, Pali and the Pastor ran high-stepping around the house through the deep, icy prairie grass.

Pali came around to the front door and went in, slamming it behind him, locking it and drawing the chain. The Pastor shook the doorknob angrily; after all, it was his home. He got the key from under the planter and unlocked the door, but the chain stopped him, "Oh gall darn, you went and did it!" he shouted. Pali watched garden clippers snip through the imitation brass door chain, then walked back up the stairs to another bedroom, closing the latch on the bedroom doorknob.

ꕥ

He was in his guest room. Gregg lay on his bed with his face in the pillow, his legs spread in a V-shape toward Pali. Gregg turned around and asked, "Would you like to smoke? I bet the Pastor decides to watch TV. He's like that, exists from one moment to the next."

It was quiet in the house. Pali could hear a Vikings football pregame talk show on the TV from the living room. He sat on the bed next to Gregg. "I made sushi for ya," said Gregg.

"Ah?" said Pali, taking some rolls from the hors d'oeuvres plate.

"Well, it's really California roll made with lefsa."

"It's good," said Pali, eating another palmful.

Gregg lit a joint and pulled a box of poppers and lube from the drawer. "We probably seem pushy to ya?" asked Gregg before holding his breath and then blowing smoke into Pali's lungs. "It's my dang dad, he acts like a kid sometimes."

"The chasing reminds me of kids," said Pali.

Gregg put aside the smoke and pushed Pali down, their tongues entangling like crazed flags. In reply, Pali pulled Gregg onto himself. He ran his palms down Gregg's curved back into his pareo, caressing his asscheeks. Gregg swiveled and ground his chest into Pali's; Pali pinched Gregg's nipples between his thumbs and forefingers. From beneath, Pali humped Gregg's groin with his own, and through their pareos their cocks tracked and slipped. Gregg's tongue beat against Pali's lips, nostrils, bridge, eyelids, into his ear, along his shoulder, into his armpit, inside his elbow, into his pareo, and finally, led by the veins, brought Pali's dick into his mouth, and slicked the cock with his spit.

Pali balanced on his elbow in the bed and turned Gregg's

body around as they each pulled the pareo from the other's body, and each fucked their cocks into the other's mouth. Pali slid on top and, arching from the root, sent the tip of his prick beyond Gregg's throat muscle, forcing him to control his breath. Gregg hummed into the head of Pali's dick. They turned and turned back on the bed, again and again, without releasing each other. The Vikings game played out downstairs, and the Pastor tossed in his chair, thinking of yet another guest one-on-one with Gregg.

Gregg pushed Pali back on the bed, his knees on either side of Pali's waist. He pressed his asshole onto Pali's standing dick and took it slowly in. Gregg's cock branched hard into Pali's sliding fist. Each inner ring of his ass opened until Pali's cock was buried deep inside. Pali's stroking blurred. Gregg's cum shot onto the wall beside the bed and ran down Pali's wrist.

Pali took Gregg's legs in his arms and brought Gregg belly down onto the bed, arching his hips into Gregg's clutching cheeks. Pali's face was empty like a runner's. Gregg's groans carried into the living room. Pali came inside Gregg's smooth, shaking ass. Then he kissed Gregg's thick shoulders, pressed his face against Gregg's, and closed his eyes.

"Our wives will be coming back from their shopping trip to Chicago tonight. It's only been a weekend, but I miss the grandchildren!" said the Pastor at breakfast the next morning. Pali watched Gregg, who was working the Sunday crossword puzzle. Before you could say, *Kafefe!* Pali was back on the freeway headed toward the towers of the Twin Cities. This time the Pastor himself drove him. Gregg stayed home, trying to repair a bicycle for one of his young daughters.

"You know, it's about time Gregg took on his own parish," said the Pastor in the car. "I'm thinking of a really nice place I know near Moscow, Minnesota."

Pali was entertaining thoughts of becoming a Buddhist. He'd met some Tibetan monks at a doll store in Stillwater. Minnesota has the largest Tibetan population in the U.S., they'd told him. "Oh what shame I will bring to my family, if I return to Samoa without a degree in Lutheran divinity!" thought Pali to himself. "Better to hide myself in this place forever, become a prostitute or a computer programmer." What other work had the seminary trained him for?

Pastor Knarffssen noted Pali's distraction and suggested they stop outside Minneapolis–St. Paul Airport to watch the jets take off. They sat silently together in the Pastor's car, parked within the repair yard fence. The planes taxied one at a time up to a turning mark near their viewpoint. Rumbling, the aircraft raced onto the field. Watching, Pali decided he would finish out the years of study he had begun, marry a nice Samoan Lutheran, build himself a Swedish sauna near Apia. He leaned back to watch the planes through the sunroof. One by one, he felt them shudder into the air and vanish.

CLAIRE TRISTRAM
When the Student Is Ready

Her first lover was big, roughly the size of her forearm. During their sex she lay still, slack-jawed and panting, focused solely on relaxing each muscle while he plowed her. If she didn't succeed in relaxing enough, he left her bleeding and barely able to sit. Every time you're naked I see something new to turn me off, he would tell her. She thought it was fun. What did she know? Long after this lover was gone from her life, she continued to fall in love with whatever man could fill her up most. And yet it seemed to her suddenly that all men were big dicks, that by having them they became them. So she gave them up, men and dicks both, to save herself.

In this period of her life she wore black. Men and women both left her alone. She became invisible to all. She could walk into a room and not a single head would turn, male or female, and she considered this indifference a sign of great accomplishment. Her body cooperated with her inclination. It stopped menstruating. The waist thickened. No one could trespass. She was impenetrable.

Only one man could have broken the long dry season of her days. Here is how he defeated her. He was fat. Not just plump, but enormously, abundantly fat, beyond all reasonable boundaries for the word, beyond the point where she recognized him as a man at all until it was too late. And he was short, at least five inches shorter than she. And bald on top of his head, but covered with hair the consistency and thickness of steel wool elsewhere. His face and neck were spackled with raised, brown moles, making him look as if he'd just been splashed with mud by a car driving through a puddle. His hygiene was poor. And he was old. All these facts conspired to keep her unaware of her own intentions until they were naked together and careening toward the abyss.

They met in a bookstore, in the health section, where she was looking for something that would explain her lack of menses, which worried her, although not too much, since she had always felt it had been her idea to stop menstruating rather than some organic problem.

"You don't need that," he said, pointing to the book in her hand. "You, honey, are in the peak of health."

She stepped back, already knocked off balance by this man. He wore trousers the size of small sails and a T-shirt that read TEXAS IS FOR LOVERS, even though they were in California. The shirt left a line of flesh exposed along the midsection. When he looked straight ahead he was looking directly at her nipples, which, to her shock, were yearning toward this unlikely target.

Why did she invite him home, then? She has an explanation, as a matter of fact. Not that she had any plan to actually touch this man. She was just curious. That was all. She wanted to understand how someone so ugly could also be so confident. She wanted to study him. Once inside he began to fondle her immediately, squeezing her breasts as if testing them for doneness. She pushed him away and laughed and said he'd gotten the wrong idea, would he like coffee? A drink? And wasn't it warm for early May? He peeled off his shirt and threw it on the floor. Such hair! He was going to shed all over. Worse. Now he let his pants drop without ceremony, leaving his naked body exposed before her like a strange primordial landscape that had no relationship to sex as she knew it.

She stood there, then, sun streaming through her kitchen window, and wondered how such an event could have happened to her, how she could find herself with such an ugly naked fat man in her kitchen. It had not been her plan. He was very fat. His great stomach, round and solid-looking, obscured any view of his cock.

Then she saw it nestling there, his little manhood, so shy, pink, so painfully small even though it was fully erect, like a snail hiding beneath the shadow of his paunch. Possibly the sight of it awoke some maternal instinct in her, for when he took her hands and drew her to him, pushing her to her knees, she didn't resist. How amazing, the audacity of it! He wasn't ashamed of his tiny thing, he was actually expecting her to worship it! He was so small, so exposed, that in her confusion she felt a kind of tenderness toward this man. There was no help for her but to eat him. She may have felt pity. Then she realized at once that she could take both the cock and the precious balls into her mouth at once, that she could enjoy the whole salad at the same time. The knowledge swept away her curiosity, her pity. She gobbled him up. Even the taste of his stale urine excited her. For the first time in her life she could appreciate the downy skin, the pulse of cock against her lips, without fear of choking on meat and cum. She milked and milked his little snail until she felt him bucking in her mouth and the sting of semen on her tongue, and she felt herself come in return, right there, kneeling on the kitchen floor.

He helped her to her feet. She stood there, not looking at him, rubbing her lips with her fingers. Do you have a bed? he asked, then followed her as she led him through the house. He undressed her without comment. So now we are both naked, she thought. Completely bare. Not touching. Suspended in that naked moment where the body has nowhere to hide. And in that naked moment she looked at him. She drank in the dense rain forest of moist and matted hair that covered the globe of his belly. She saw the flesh that hung like slabs from his shoulders. She saw him looking at her, too, at her mismatched tits, her imperfect thighs, the jagged scar of her appendectomy. Not evaluating her. Appreciating her. She could somehow feel the difference, even though he said nothing, even though she didn't know his name. His breasts were as big as hers. His legs were thin, old man's legs, almost too fragile to hold his mass.

"You are glowing," he said.

She could feel herself glowing, as a matter of fact. She could feel her body giving off radiant heat as he looked at her.

"Have you done this before?" he said as he began to kiss her.

Done what before? she wondered, but said yes, because anything else sounded like a lie.

Then his hand touched her stomach and her body stopped glowing, abruptly. The light went out and all was darkness and chaos and despair. She pushed him back onto the bed to hide her sudden shame, the pain that always came when she was naked with a man. Any man. Even him. The hurting truth of her own imperfections descended on her. She was buried under all the feelings she had hoped and prayed and failed to avoid by choosing to be naked with this particular man, this grotesque.

To distract herself she began to fuck him, or at least to try. His stomach was too large and his cock too small. She couldn't manage it. He smiled at her fumblings and made soothing sounds in the back of his throat. He drew her down on the bed and rested her head on his meaty shoulder. He stroked her hair. She grew restless again, uneasy. Things weren't progressing as planned. They should have been doing it by now. She wanted to. She'd made the decision and now she wanted to follow through. The knot of tension was growing ever larger between her legs. She didn't question it any longer.

"Do I excite you?" he asked her.

Yesyesyesyes, oh yes, she said, although she didn't believe it until later.

He raised his head and looked at her. His face was as big as God's. Then his great mass rose up, until he was over her, inconceivably huge, like Mother Earth herself. He will crush me, she thought, and didn't care. He spread her legs and pulled her, ah, it could be done! onto his prick, his little pizzicato, his feather-finger. She came as he entered her.

He began to rock. He stretched her wide, as far as she could open, to accommodate his mighty circumference. His stomach, that huge and hairy globe, rubbed and pounded every inch of her from her center to her knees, while his prick danced in and out like a tongue. When she grew too wet and wide to hold him inside he fell out of her, and it didn't matter, nothing mattered, because he kept rubbing her until they both peaked again, when, exhausted and spent, they fell asleep within each other's arms.

Weeks later, when she knew even more about his body than before, when he'd probed her in ways that would have been cruelly painful with any of her former lovers, when she trusted him, she awoke to find them both covered in her menstrual blood. The long dry season had ended. He opened his eyes and told her she was beautiful, and she knew that it was true.

They stayed together for a long time, until he gave her crabs. He denied nothing. "She needed me, too," he told her. Her fury at his honesty made him repulsive again. Once more she could see the sagging breasts, the vast and sweaty geography of skin and hair and fat that was his body. He disgusted her. She threw him out. Then bought gallons, oceans, of Kwell. She disinfected herself and her house for many weeks. Afterward, she wore white.

Years passed. The woman lost track of the man. But she would wonder about him sometimes. What was he to her, then? An ugly man. A former lover. A cheat. A freak. All of those things. Or none of them. In truth she had difficulty remembering. Usually when she thought of him she could think of nothing but the crabs, and her lips would recite a prayer of vengeance: May he tone up, thin down, become average and unremarkable, because then he will have lost everything.

But sometimes, more often lately than before, she will find herself rising above her anger, to a place where she can think about the man himself instead of just his sins. At those times, she finds a prayer of thanks forming on her lips.

Thank you, wherever you are, she whispers. Thank you for showing me the beauty of imperfect things.

Like you.

Like me.

JAMES WILLIAMS
Jason's Cock

What I love most about Jason's cock is not its size but its grace, in every sense. I like to lie with my cheek on his belly and introduce myself to it over and over again, getting to know it for the first time every time, brushing it over my eyes, my cheeks, my nose, my mouth, trailing it down my throat inside and out. It always stands up for me like a sentinel, ready to serve, eager to please. The skin is soft and smooth as a tropical breeze signaling monsoons in days to come. It darkens and flushes, pales, darkens and flushes again as if it were a special landscape of flesh the clouds pass over on their way to rain. It smells like a summer beach at sunset after a long day of lying in hot sand anticipating everything forbidden. It pulses slowly with the steady beat of his life and sometimes with a less steady beat of its own, and if I press it with my finger underneath his balls it dances like a lap dog, and his balls begin to steal away as if they're tiptoeing out the door at midnight when they promised to stay home at ten, and if I rest my ear against his sac I can hear the single odd-nailed floorboard creak with almost every other step.

The way it arches like a well-strung bow brings back the fantasies I used to have of sucking cock when I was still too young to have really tried. I thought I'd find another boy who'd somehow be staying in a house nearby when we were on vacation at the lake in Michigan. I'd see him on the beach one day, and even though we wouldn't say a word I'd know that he'd seen me as well. Dusk would fall, and then full night. My family would go to sleep and I'd go out for a moonlight walk. The air would still be warm from the day, and the lake would be so flat the moon and her entire history would lie across its missing ripples like silver two-dimensional apples. There would still be frogs and crickets in those days, fireflies would glitter like tiny spotlights caught on distant tinsel tassels, the grass above the sand would be wet with early dew. I would have no way to know that he was there and still I'd walk along the grass and underneath a tree right into his arms and we would kiss until we fell down from the weight of memory, knowing already how our lives would fit. Somehow our clothes just disappeared, and I made him cry out with desire as I milked him with my mouth but took myself away before he came and made him stop, and made him count from ten to one aloud and slowly before I swallowed his balls and let them try to slip from between my thinly parted lips, ran my tongue like a swift snake down his root to where it disappeared inside his body, and licked him where the hot lake had not dried yet.

I tongue his Rimbaldian fawn-brown pucker and come

back in a swallow to this graceful instrument that looks now like a stretching cat caught in a moment it cannot relieve.

Jason is so wet I could fuck myself on him without any lube, but I'm not nearly ready to let him come so close to coming. I have only just begun to worship, I have just begun to let my tongue get slippery in all that moisture, pushing it into the little hole that opens and opens and opens for me to fuck it but is still too small, so I suck him up instead and feel his head get harder and hotter and I know he's ready so I slide him out from between my tightened lips and back away again just as I did with the boy at the lake, and watch him throb before my eyes enfolded now in nothing but this wind I've whipped up with my breath to blow on him, to cool him down, to slow his movement that he wants and needs and thinks is inevitable, letting him show me now how much he's learned because he knows he doesn't have permission yet, I haven't said *good boy now you can come,* I haven't finished yet with Jason's cock. There is this little line, this little crimp of pleated skin, below his head in front that leads me down to where his hard soft shaft is so translucent I imagine I can see the muscle filling and emptying, this little line that leads me away from his small hole and down the thick blue vein I want to bite into so I can drink his hidden blood while he comes, and so I nibble now a little letting Jason know that I have teeth and that I am not using them, not yet, not as fully as I could, and when he shakes so hard his thighs and belly tremble but he still does not come then I know that he has understood.

This other vein that runs along the side reminds me more of rope and so remembering the first boy I ever tied to my bed I lick that rope on Jason while he tries to keep from screaming. The boy was probably a virgin, and he let on that he was straight. I brought him home on the pretense that he'd like to

see the black-and-yellow butterfly I'd chloroformed and
pinned to a white board under glass. He was not the kind of
boy who pulled the wings off flies but I was. I showed him the
butterfly but made him beg to see it first, and when he'd
begged me hard enough I told him he could only see it if he
took off his shirt, and then his pants, and then all his clothes.
He was obviously scared and just as obviously excited, his
pants when I told him about the shirt were standing out and
dark with his wet precum. Then he was naked in my bedroom
with just a few tan public hairs and a cock very much like Jason's only younger, curved and graceful as a sonatina, so I
showed him the butterfly and stood behind him pressing up
against his ass while he examined every minute vein and curl
on the butterfly's wing as if he were a fascinated lepidopterist
who did not even notice he was naked in my gaze. I put my
arms around him to show him what the butterfly looked like
upside down and sideways, and worked my way up his belly
to his tits with one hand while I worked my own pants down
and off rubbing my dick against his butt as hard and round as
a twelve-year-old baking bowl. That was the day I learned I
didn't have to come if I didn't want to because I made myself
stop so what we were doing could go on into the afternoon.

He turned to face me when I was naked too and I kissed
him, took the butterfly away and set it on my dresser where it
wouldn't get hurt, then took his arms in my two hands and
pushed them behind him and held them there while I hugged
him to me and kissed him the way I wanted to kiss the boy on
the beach beside the lake at night, only this one was alive and
kissed me back. I pushed him backward toward the bed and
pushed him down on his back and stood over him astonished
at what God had suddenly given me, as I am astonished now
rubbing Jason's sweet cock up and down with my hungry

tongue as fast as I can move my head while his hips buck up and down shoving his dick into space searching for relief while his balls roll free. I take those fat nuggets in my empty hand and slowly slowly slowly start to squeeze them ever so slightly gently but more and more firmly, painfully, harder, press them because he knows I want to burst their bloody juices in my hand, and I work my tongue around the head of his cock again and again while he slaps at the bed, at his own thigh, and pinch it just exactly underneath the head front and back anytime I think he's getting too close for my own comfort, slow him down and speed him up at once, which is what I did to the boy on my childhood bed.

I smiled at him as if I knew what I was doing, took the clothesline I'd been saving for what I didn't know till then, and tied a noose around his balls and tied them tightly to his ankles so he had to bend his knees and looked at me with fear that was almost horror and made me want to laugh. I tied his hands together to the bedpost then and said I wanted to watch him come. I spit in my hand and greased his ass and fucked him while I pulled him off and just kept fucking him while his ass rings squeezed my dick and he gushed all over the sheet and when he cried because he didn't know what else to do I came as well, came up his ass and lost my dick in him and lost myself. Later I untied him except for the noose on his balls and the rope I had attached to them that I held like a leash while he looked up at me like a happy puppy and fell asleep in my arms until my mother called up the stairs that it was dinnertime. I got him up in the early evening light and we got dressed, he kissed me and went home alone, and I never even saw him in school again.

Jason, on the other hand, will never leave because I never let him come until he's passed the point of wanting to. I like it when he cries because he's just so full he cannot stand to have me near his dick and I don't even want to pause to breathe, I want to drink the smell and sound and taste and sight and feel of him down into me until he fills me up, which he can never do, and so it's easy for me to keep him on the edge as long as I want and he knows it is my right to do it, my right to command him to come or command him not to come and let him sleep with his blue balls for a month, but I have never been pointlessly mean, I just like him to know who's boss and that is what he begs me for, crawling down the corridor on his knees and manacled hands some days after I've been lunching on his straining cock while the sun moved gradually across the patient sky, dragging his shackled ankles chained to his steel-collared balls from the kitchen where I've sent him for a glass of water just because I can and back into the living room where I'm leaning against the far arm of the couch watching traffic in the street two floors below.

The woman who lives across the narrow courtyard, old enough to be his mother, is standing in her window the way she's done for weeks when I come into the living room bare-assed, I think she thinks she's hidden by her lacy drapery and that I can't see she's got her own hand up her skirt I know she'll have off long before I'm done with Jason crawling toward me in his chains, bringing with him not only the glass of water but also his pretty penis dick-a-dangle heavy hot-hung hook of hulking manflesh ramrod pigtool Lenny Bruce's thick fuckin' pile-drivin' fist at the end of a baby's arm O! so sweet and graceful cock I want to rip it from his body and carry it with me in my mouth next to my heart, take it out and look at it on the subway suck on it and show it off, honey cock I dream about from time to time like a blimp taking up my entire sky, like a love fat baby I rock in my arms, like a stag I run down and mount, like the whole loved life that Jason reminds me is here before it's too late and gone.

No one else saw the stag, they were off chasing some other forest thing, and I was too young to know that killing it would haunt me and I didn't run it down, I shot it *blam* between the eyes the first and only time I shot the rifle Dad had given me and it fell backward as if some atomic blast had knocked it over, not a little piece of lead that happened to find its way across a chasm of experience. By the time I reached its side its eyes were fluttering but it was still alive and looked at me. I had never been so hard in all my life and I forgot the other people in the woods, dropped my rifle, dropped my pants and sank myself into it while it died. The spirit of a god passed out from between its lips in a rushing gasp of flight, its eyes went empty and we were nothing else but flesh together except that I was still alive. I climbed off and pulled up my pants before I got too scared to stay and no one ever knew I killed the stag, they'd all shot another deer and that was all they cared about, soon we all went home and soon thereafter I threw away the gun.

Jason is a little like a stag sometimes in his muscles and his brow but he is docile now because I have his balls wrapped up so tightly in my fist and I am looking murder in his eyes, I bare my teeth, he knows I want to kill him with my dick because I cannot stand how much I love him, I look at his penis pleading for release but he's stopped bucking, he's stopped moving he has stopped believing altogether I will let him have relief and only tears are rolling down his cheeks, which means I think the time has come. I pull his balls and punch him with the hand I hold them in until he yells so loudly that the woman whose skirt is gone is startled, and I take his whole cock down my throat and swallow it again and again until he starts to beg again and call me *Sir* and *Sir* and *Sir please Sir please ow ow ow Sir please Sir please Sir please may I come* and I say word by word as I bring him all the way out of my mouth, *On the count of three you may come, yes, you may come, yes, one, two, three,* and he shouts and cries and screams and my face and throat are wet-hot and spunky and poor Jason shivers and shakes like a dying old jalopy and comes some more and finally starts calming down and bends himself into a little ball and commences sobbing in my arms. When he's fully quiet and starting to doze I turn him softly on his belly and use his own gism and my own spit as lube, settle myself deep in his ass and pull up gently on his hair. He raises his ass to meet me as I move and starts to move himself up and down for me while I ride on his hipbones and watch his hole darken as he takes me in, then pink up as he lets me out, darken and pink, darken and pink. I remember the first time that I fucked Jason and how I will fuck him again and again just as long as forever, knowing I will never stop until I have done the impossible and satisfied myself with the grace of his cock in every sense. I ride and I ride and I ride, holding myself in check until he's rasping and shoving himself back on me, clawing at the sheets and I can feel his asshole twitch, and then at last at last I let myself go.

M. J. ROSE
From *Lip Service*

What do you want your name to be?" Candy asked.

We were sitting in her office. She was sipping espresso, and I was holding my hands together so she wouldn't see them shaking.

"Does every phone therapist have a pseudonym?" I asked.

Candy said they did. "First for protection, but also because for some of us it's easier to separate and become someone else on the phone."

"Alice," I responded, surprised at how easily I had chosen the name. Alice. I could see her. Alice was my graduate student. Able to see the wonder in this new world. Alice, who was bright, brave, and just bad enough to enjoy all this.

For the next twenty minutes, Candy briefed me on my first caller. "Bill and his wife were patients here for several years," she explained. "He's an extremely large man and his wife found it painful to have intercourse with him. After many years of rejection, he developed performance problems and they turned to us. In addition to other therapies, we used phone therapy with Bill to help rebuild his confidence. He's no longer a patient, but he's become a client."

I wanted to know more about the case, but Candy said everything else was confidential unless Sam decided otherwise. "Just remember, Bill's at a stage where he likes to direct his fantasies. All you have to do is be accepting and giving. He's a special man, Julia. So relax. Everything will be fine," she said, as she set me up in the same room where I'd been practicing calls. I settled back in the big armchair with the phone in front of me. From speakers in the ceiling, gentle classical music took the edge off the silence. And then a few minutes after Candy shut the door behind her, the phone rang.

⚬

"Hello," I said, croaking out the word.

The man on the other end responded with his own hello.

"Bill?" I asked, trying to keep my voice from cracking.

"Yes. Is this Alice?"

And with my eyes shut and the phone in my hand, it was. "Yes, this is Alice."

"So you're new?" Bill asked.

"Uh-huh. How'd you know?"

"Candy told me about you. Are you nervous?" His voice was rich and lyrical.

I laughed. "Oh boy, am I nervous. Can't you hear my heart beating over the phone?"

"Well, you don't have to be nervous with me. You know, you have a very gentle voice."

"Thank you."

"My back was to the door when you walked in because I

was talking to another juror, so I didn't see you, but I heard you ask if this was grand jury room number two. Your voice made me turn around. I was so pleased when you took the empty seat beside me. You've never been on a grand jury before, have you?"

"No." From what I'd learned in training, he was leading me into a fantasy he'd already begun. All I had to do was pay attention and pick up his clues.

"So you didn't know that once you sat down, that would be your seat for the whole month?"

"No. But . . . when I saw you next to me, I was glad."

"Why is that?" Bill asked.

"Because . . . because of how wonderful you smelled. I kept breathing it in, hoping you wouldn't notice."

"I wish you'd told me. Is that why you stayed and talked to me during the break?" he asked.

"Yes. I wanted to get closer to that smell."

"I hope I'm not disturbing you, at home like this. I mean, it was kind of sneaky how I got your number—telling you each jury member should have another member's number in case you couldn't get through to the bailiff."

"Isn't that why you're calling? To tell me we don't have to show up for jury duty tomorrow or something?" I asked.

"No. Is it all right I called?" he asked.

"Yes."

"Your boyfriend isn't there, is he?"

"No, he's away."

"He travels often, doesn't he?"

I hesitated. "Yes." The introduction of a boyfriend confused me.

"And leaves you lonely?"

"Yes, he leaves me lonely," I answered.

"What do you do to keep yourself busy when he's away?"

"Watch a lot of old movies."

I answered before realizing that was exactly what I was doing now that Paul was traveling and working late so often.

"Do you cry at the end?" he asked.

"Always."

"If I was with you and you started to cry, I would brush away your tears with my lips," he whispered into the phone.

I was strangely moved by the image. "No one has ever done that before," I said, again telling the truth.

"Are there other things no one has ever done to you that you'd like me to do?"

Bill was taking shape in my mind. Not as a face, but as sensations, colors. He was dark blue velvet. Heavy cream. A large bird flying through a moonless sky.

"Yes. Are there things no one has done to you?" I asked.

"No, I want to know about you," he answered quickly.

I must have taken a wrong step.

"What do you want that your boyfriend doesn't give you?" He put the focus back on me.

A moment passed. I couldn't think of what to say.

"Alice?" he prompted, and she responded for me.

"He never makes love to me long enough," I answered finally.

"I will," he said. "Where should I start?"

If only he'd talk about his fantasy. This was so difficult for me to do. And then I realized this was his fantasy: to please a woman, to please me. After that, it was easier.

"We'd both be completely dressed, sitting on my couch. There'd be just one light on. And you'd kiss me. Keep on kissing me—"

"So that you could almost come from the kiss?" he asked.

"Yes," I whispered, surprised that nothing about this make-believe conversation was repulsive or frightening. I was in my head where I'd been so many times before, only now there was another voice in my fantasy.

"Alice, have you ever come from a kiss?"

"No."

"That's what I'm going to do to you now. I'm going to make you come from kissing you. Would you like that?" Bill asked.

"If you kiss me for that long, your lips will be sore."

"I don't care. I want to rub my lips on yours. Wet and slippery. And so, so soft. Can you feel it?"

"Yes," I said, and I could.

"I'm unbuttoning your blouse and pushing it off your shoulders so I can kiss your breasts. So I can suck on your nipples," he said.

"Your lips are like feathers on my skin. Bill, are you hard?"

I'd been trained to ask this question often to gauge whether the call was working; if a man wasn't hard after a few minutes, something was wrong.

"I'm very hard," he said, and I segued into the next stage of the conversation.

"Are you touching yourself, Bill?"

"Yes, I'm rubbing myself while I imagine kissing you. I want to keep on kissing you. Alice, tell me how it feels."

"Wonderful. Our lips are so wet they glide against each other."

"Uh-huh," he murmured.

"And your tongue darts out—oh—it's hard—like your cock." It was my voice, but it was Alice who was thinking up the words.

"Oh . . ." His breathing had changed.

From the tapes Candy had played for me, I was familiar

with this transition. At a certain point, usually minutes from orgasm, a man's breathing changes and his responses become shorter and less coherent.

"Your tongue parts my lips and slips inside my mouth where it's warm and wet. And then just as I start to suck on your tongue, you pull back and withdraw," I said.

"But . . . you go after me . . . ," he told me.

"Yes . . . I grab on to your tongue with my teeth and draw it back into my mouth. Your tongue fills up my whole mouth."

"Suck on it . . . suck . . . on my tongue . . . ," he pleaded.

"Yes . . . I'm sucking on it, going up and down on your tongue. It's filling up my whole mouth. I let you slip almost all the way out and then suck you back inside again. God, I wish your tongue could come, right now, inside my mouth," I whispered.

"Ohh . . . God . . ."

⑥

It was the first time I'd really listened to a man come. Not seen him and felt him, but heard his release through the sounds he made.

"Was it all right?" I asked, suddenly shy.

Bill sounded content. "Yes . . . yes, it was wonderful, but next time, I want to make you come too. All right, Alice?"

He'd thrown me off balance.

"Yeah. Okay. Good-bye, Bill." I shivered and hung up the phone.

DAMIAN GRACE
The Man Who Ate Women

I don't drink much these days, but five years ago, when this tawdry incident happened, I was at a time in my life when I drank heavily almost every night. The prevailing wisdom in my social circle was that you couldn't have a good time without alcohol, and we all considered ourselves harmless social drinkers. If you'd asked me the definition of an antisocial drinker, I guess I'd have described someone who throws up on your shoes or crosses the double yellow line and turns you into roadkill. Anyway, the point I'm trying to make is that I was loaded.

It happened at one of John Kindle's infamous weekly house parties, the ones where he would invite maybe a dozen people and fifty or sixty people would show up. Kindle was a college buddy of mine who had told us all that the Internet was going to be the Next Big Thing. We had ignored his advice while he was busy putting his money where his mouth was, and now he never had to work again.

I was a regular guest, and while you never knew everyone, I had enough buddies, male and female, to feel relaxed and comfortable. The atmosphere was a sort of postcollege hip thing—people two or five or even ten years out of school trying to recapture the feeling of freedom and belonging of those undergraduate days.

Dressing down was the absolute rule. The guy in the muscle shirt and hightops might be a corporate lawyer on the fast track to partner, and the woman in the tie-dyed shirt and clogs could easily be a buttoned-down drone with Anderson Consulting. I was in grad school at the time, so as I saw it I had a right to wear loose jeans and sandals and a LEGALIZE POT T-shirt.

There was plenty of sex at these parties. Not as much as you might hear about the next day, of course, but I know how to separate fact from bragging, and there was plenty of fact. All those people trooping up and down the stairs to the second floor weren't inspecting Kindle's famous record collection or checking out the new wallpaper in his study.

I guess I got about my fair share. I didn't try as hard as some guys, and sometimes that works out better anyway. My God, with guys like Jerry Shaughnessy or Guido the Italian Stallion, if they didn't have a real solid line on some trim by ten or eleven you could see the panic in their eyes, like a hunter on the last day of deer season. My normal pattern was to wait until things thinned out a bit, maybe one A.M. or so, and then take a casual look around to see who might be available. Lately it had been Amy Hauder more often than not, and I sensed I might be drifting into a relationship in my usual aimless way.

We were down in the basement, where the laid-back cool

regulars hung out, and the conversation was moving right along. Just the right mix of edgy critical people like Jennifer Chase and Seth Jabovic to stir the pot, and type-B conciliators like me and Doris and Amira to calm things down and smooth over ruffled feathers when the pot started to boil over.

You can just about set your watch by the topics. From nine to ten it's all gossipy chitchat: "Did you ever meet . . . ?" and "Did you hear what so-and-so did last week?"—that sort of thing. When that gets old we move on to politics and issues of the day. Imagine a younger McLaughlin Group sitting around in beanbag chairs with drinks in their hands, smoking up a storm.

Once the budget is balanced, the trickier foreign policy issues have been settled, and pot is legal and available in every supermarket, the boy-girl thing finally bubbles to the surface. Call it midnight. And once you get on the topic of sex and relationships you never get off it, because nothing ever gets settled in *that* area.

We had more gals than guys in the circle that night—Jimmy and Big Herman were at a Blackhawks game, I think. The previous night there had been a strange incident at one of the fraternities on the local campus, and the rumors were flying.

"It's called a train," said Seth. He waved a thin white hand dismissively, sending a trail of smoke floating upward. "Disgusting, really, but certainly not a crime."

"Sounds like the police think it was a crime," said Jennifer. "I heard they dragged a bunch of hungover frat guys in for questioning."

Seth shrugged. "Of course, if the woman files a complaint afterward, they have to investigate."

"Investigate what?" asked Amy. "Can someone tell me what the hell a 'train' is?"

"A gang-bang, of sorts," said Seth. He pushed back a lock of dark, lank hair and went into professor mode. "A woman at a party decides she wants to take on all comers. She'll go into a room, and the guys will line up outside the door to take their turn. A whole train of guys, one after the other."

"But why?" asked Amy helplessly.

"I don't know, you tell me," said Seth. "Must be a deep-down female fantasy."

"I don't think so," said Doris, and other girls shook their heads as well. "It's repulsive."

"Lack of self-esteem, probably," said Jennifer. "Some girls get so brainwashed by our male-dominated society that they equate putting out with being popular."

This was a typical Jennifer Chase troll, and everyone ignored it.

Brad shifted in his beanbag and said, "I was in a bar once and a girl got up on a stool and announced she was going to give a blowjob to every guy there. She said she lost some kind of bet, but obviously that was just a silly excuse."

Jennifer raised an eyebrow. "And?"

He shrugged sheepishly. "What do you think? I was like third in line, out of a dozen. It's not like she was wasted or high or something—she knew what she was doing."

Jennifer snorted. "Oh, so then it's okay."

Brad looked embarrassed. "So what, you think I shouldn't have?"

"I wouldn't expect anything different from a man."

"I can't believe a woman would ever do that," said Amy. "So demeaning."

I spoke up. "If she does it of her own free will, and on her terms, is it really demeaning? I mean, if she has a fantasy about a gang-bang or whatever, can't you give her credit for feeling liberated enough to act on it?"

Several people spoke at once. Fatefully, it was Jennifer who raised her voice and continued to speak.

"How can you think a woman could really enjoy something like that? How would you like performing oral sex on a dozen women you hardly know, one right after the other?"

I felt a little lurch in my stomach. Back then, I had a sort of policy of always speaking my mind and telling the truth, no matter what. I think I was under the influence of some subversive writer. Walt Whitman, or maybe it was Ayn Rand.

"I'd love it," I said. "This may shock you, but that happens to be a deep dark fantasy of mine."

There was a predictable round of laughter. They all thought I was kidding, except for Seth, who isn't easily fooled.

"It might be dark, but it isn't deep anymore, Steve-O," said Seth. "It's right up here on the surface where we can poke it."

"Very funny, Steve," said Amira in her faint Hindi accent. "But really, come on."

"I'm serious," I said. "Really. So it doesn't seem so odd to me that a woman might fantasize about the same thing."

In a loud voice, Jennifer said, "You're telling me, you would go up to one of the bedrooms right now, and we could go announce to everyone you were going to . . . going to do a . . ."

"Taco train?" suggested Brad.

"Oh, very nice, Brad. A cunnilingus train, and you would service any woman who went up there?"

"Sure," I said. "But no women would go for it. You chicks are all so dainty and refined. Only men have the sturdy mental outlook required to take advantage of free, no-strings-attached sex."

"You're lying," said Amira. "I bet you wouldn't do it." Her voice was accusing, but I noticed a twinkle in her brown eyes.

"Oh, I bet he would," said Seth, winking at me. "Don't underestimate our Steve. He's right, though. None of you women would have the guts to take him up on it. Unless maybe if he was blindfolded, so he couldn't see who he was eating. . . ."

I felt my cock start to worm its way down the leg of my jeans like it had a life of its own.

Amy said "Let me get this straight—Steve would be lying blindfolded on the bed, and we would just go in there anonymously and sit on his face?"

"And if he correctly identifies all the women by taste alone, he wins a special prize," said Seth, ever the wit.

"A case of Scope," said Amira, and everyone laughed.

"It's an amusing idea," said Jennifer. "But I guarantee he won't get any takers."

"Only one way to find out," said Seth.

Jennifer looked at me challengingly. "What do you say, Steve?"

I swallowed hard. "Is the blindfold necessary?"

There was a chorus of yesses and nods.

They were all looking at me. Seth and Brad were amused, of course. Jennifer, the sturdy field hockey player with the firm jaw and blue eyes, looked triumphant, like she was about to win an argument. Amy, the skinny blonde who was the only one I had gone down on before, looked embarrassed. Mindy and Doris just looked curious. Amira was the only one who looked like she was turned on by the idea. When our eyes met, she dropped hers and smiled.

"Let's do it," I said.

"Good man!" said Seth with a chuckle.

I went up to the second floor with Seth and Jennifer, who seemed to be the self-appointed referees for each gender. We found an empty bedroom and cleared the coats off the bed. Seth found a scarf and tied it around my head, almost burning me with his cigarette in the process. He left a generous gap at the bottom, and I could look down and see my shoes.

"Can you see anything?" asked Jennifer.

"Not really. You want to go first?"

"No way. I'm going to go tell all the women it's free head, no conversation needed. We'll see if you get any customers." They left, turning out the overhead light and leaving the room in semidarkness. I went over to the bed and lay down, moving awkwardly with the blindfold. Nothing happened for a while, and I started regretting the whole thing. Ever since I hit puberty and the hormones started to rage, I'd been fascinated by the idea of eating pussy. It seemed like such a perverse, unnatural thing to do, and yet it had such potential to give pleasure to women.

Ah, women. Fascinating, ethereal creatures, superior to men, or at least to boys, in every way. Able to humble us with a sly look or a toss of the hair. They seemed to have some ancient knowledge passed down to them regarding relationships and men and sex, so that a girl of thirteen or fourteen somehow possessed the accumulated wisdom of generations, while we boys had to flounder and blush and stammer as we slowly figured things out for ourselves. But it seemed to me that these godlike creatures had an Achilles' heel, and that it was the very thing that was also the source of their power.

I sensed from a young age the uneasy relationship women had with their genitals. They were ashamed of the way they looked down there, and the way they smelled, and tasted. They couldn't understand how men could be attracted to the oozing slot between their legs like bees to a ripe, pollen-heavy flower.

To nuzzle between the legs of one of these creatures was to upset the balance of power. It was to worship at the altar of womanhood, and at the same time it was to strike a rebellious blow against the all-powerful spell that held men in the thrall of women. If you were sucking a woman's cunt, you were sacrificing yourself for her, and yet she was in your power.

As I matured, I naturally discovered that things weren't quite so dramatic. Women weren't all-knowing creatures after all, and they weren't the enemy. They were subject to base desires and cravings just like men. But like so many things that affect us strongly when we are young and malleable, my fixation remained long after the worldview that shaped it had shifted. I still craved the act of joining my mouth and tongue to a woman's secret musky inner regions. It was submission and power combined, and it was my constant fantasy.

But lying there alone in the dim bedroom, I was having second thoughts. Some fantasies should remain just that, and I was almost relieved that no women were taking me up on the offer. A few more minutes and I could rip off the blindfold and claim a political victory.

There was a thump outside the door, barely audible over the bass vibration from the big speakers downstairs. Two female voices, each trying to shush the other.

The door opened, brightening the room, and I swallowed hard. Drunk female laughter, and then the door closed again.

"He's in there!"

"I told you. Now go on . . ." The rest was muffled.

This is humiliating, I thought. I'm out of here.

The door opened again, and this time they came in and shut it behind them. I could hear their heavy breathing as they looked at me.

"Hi," I said.

"Party Girl here wants to sit on your face," said one. "I'm just her chaperone." This struck them as funny, and they both broke into choked laughter.

"Is that what you want?" asked Party Girl. "I mean . . . really?"

"I lost a bet."

"Oh . . . okay. So it's not like you really want to . . . "

It would be easy to say something that would get me off the hook. Even through a haze of alcohol, she was hesitant about inflicting her cunt on a stranger.

"No, I want to. Besides, I can't settle the bet until I actually get a bunch of women to sit on my face."

"Shit, what the hell, then. Is the door locked?"

"Yep," said the chaperone.

I heard the rustling of clothing, and then the bed shifted sharply. Through the crack in the blindfold I could see she was wearing a short skirt, which she had rolled up around her waist. All she had taken off were her panties, and maybe her shoes. Her thighs nestled on either side of my head, and I caught the first whiff of her pussy. It was pungent, with a faint undertone of urine, but not unpleasant. She had probably showered before the party, but had of course been dancing and drinking since then.

She kneed me painfully in the ear, apologized, and then her pussy was in my face.

I licked up at her awkwardly, pushing my tongue into the damp folds. The taste was tangy, the smell stronger now. Pubic hairs tickled my nose. For the first few minutes it didn't go very well. I couldn't really reach her clit without straining my neck, and she kept squirming around, alternately pulling away and then mashing her cunt into my face as she tried to get comfortable on the soft mattress.

"Hold on a sec," she said.

She wedged a pillow under my head and then scooched forward a bit. Then she sat back down, lowering her pussy into just the right position. Dinner is served, I thought. I dove back into her wet and pleasantly musky cunt, and went to work on her clit. Before long she was grinding herself gently against my mouth in a pleasantly familiar rhythm.

"He's good at this, Cheryl," she said huskily, forgetting about staying anonymous.

"Oh yeah? Are you going to come?" Cheryl the chaperone's voice was teasing.

"Maybe . . ."

About a minute later she did, with a short, high-pitched groan that was equal parts surprise and pleasure. Putting modesty aside for a moment, I'm really very good at eating pussy.

She rolled off me, giving me a needed breath of air, and then she kissed me briefly on the lips and said, "Thanks, stranger."

Cheryl was laughing. "You little slut, I can't believe you just came on his face!"

Emboldened by my success, I said, "I bet I can do the same thing for you."

"I wish I was wearing a skirt," she said. "Maybe I would. But I'm not taking my pants off."

"You can wear my skirt, and I'll put on your jeans," said Party Girl.

There was a moment of silence. Cheryl had clearly been trapped.

"Sit on my face," I said. "I promise you won't regret it."

"Well hell, I guess it's just one of those nights my Mama warned me about," said Cheryl. I heard the welcome sound of a zipper going down. Some rustling and giggling, and then another warm shape looming above me, and another unique fragrance.

Cheryl's pussy wasn't as pungent as her friend's, but it was amazingly wet. As I stroked my tongue up her slot, her puffy lips opened, releasing a warm gush of pussy cream that soon was running down my chin.

"Oh wow," said Cheryl. "Stranger, you sure know how to make a girl feel good."

"Told you so," said Party Girl.

Cheryl settled herself in more firmly, and the world narrowed down to a wet pussy, a firm little nub, and my tongue. Somewhere above me, Cheryl started saying, "Oh . . . oh . . . oh . . ." at regular intervals. My cock was a constant throbbing lump in my pants, far in the opposite direction.

When she came, she tensed up and became completely still, an orgasmic response that was uncommon but not rare. I loved it, because it allowed me to sense the minute changes in her physiology—the sudden thickening of her outer lips, the swelling and even the quivering of her clitoris.

"Oh fuck yes!" said Cheryl. We were both gasping for air. "That was a fucking ride!"

"I want to go again," said Party Girl. "Shit, what I really want to do is take this guy home and chain him to my bed."

"I'm supposed to serve all comers," I said. "But if no one else is waiting . . ."

As if on cue, there was a knock at the door.

My two new friends swore under their breath and pulled themselves together. Then there was a low-pitched conversation at the door.

"Guess what?" called Party Girl.

"A line around the block?" I ventured.

"Not quite, I mean, women aren't quite so bold as to stand in line, but the word is that you've got some more customers waiting."

"Better send 'em in, then."

And in they came, in a continuous stream, sometimes alone, more often in groups of two. I ate pussy steadily for the next two hours, or so they told me later. As far as I was concerned, time pretty much lost meaning.

How many? I honestly don't know. At least twenty. Twenty new pussies: twenty new smells, twenty new tastes. There were cunts so hairy that it was like eating out a broom, which was sort of a drag, and there were a few that were shaved slick and bare, which isn't really my preference either. There were small cunts with tightly folded lips that had to be teased open with a rigid tongue tip, and big cunts with soft lips that enveloped my tongue and nose in a warm, musky embrace.

Some of the women were obviously just doing it on a dare, and they would just climb on and then back off after a cursory tonguing. One women was so drunk that she kept losing her balance and falling off the bed—the second time that happened I sent her away. Of those that actually allowed themselves to get into it, I was able to make about two out of three come, which I thought was pretty damn good under the circumstances.

One girl ground her pussy into my face for about ten minutes straight, stranded in the lonely territory just short of orgasm, swearing like a sailor and gasping out instructions that I followed to the letter. Despite our best efforts she was simply unable to come.

"I'm just too fucking drunk," she said finally, with endearing honesty. She was close to tears with frustration. "Don't take this personally. . . ."

She lifted herself up a few inches off my face and started rubbing herself. I watched through the ever-growing gap in my blindfold, fascinated, as her fingers savagely rubbed and pulled at her cunt. When I sensed she was finally about to come, I slid down and jabbed my tongue up into her slick hole as far as I could. She let out a guttural shriek and went off like a Roman candle. She was one of the women who insisted on giving me her phone number.

The door opened, and someone came in and loosened my blindfold. I found myself looking up at Amira.

"How's the man of the hour?" she asked. "The gang wants to know how you're holding up. Jennifer Chase wants me to tell you she's going to have to reconsider her entire worldview because of this."

I smiled at her and sat up. "My face is sticky, my neck is stiff, and my tongue and jaw are exhausted. Other than that I'm great."

"I thought you might be working up a thirst," she said, holding out a cup of beer.

I took the cup gratefully and downed it in one long, delicious gulp. "God, I needed that."

She chuckled, her teeth showing white against her dark skin. "Ready to get back to it?"

"Actually, I think I've had enough."

"Aw, too bad. I guess I'm too late, then."

"I didn't realize you were here as a customer," I said, looking at her with new interest. Amira was one of those women who are all curves, and she looked too young to be in law school. Dark, arched eyebrows over liquid brown eyes, full red lips, a round face framed by thick wavy hair. Full breasts, round hips and thighs, but a surprisingly narrow waist. My cock, which had been up and down all night, began hardening again.

She sat down next to me, and said, "Steve, I just wanted to say that you've got a lot of guts acting out your fantasy like this."

"You think so?"

She dropped her eyes, and said, "Please don't tell anyone, but I have a similar fantasy. Like the girl at the fraternity the other night."

"You want to be train fucked? You're kidding!" The idea of sweet, quiet Amira taking on a whole fraternity seemed beyond crazy, and I couldn't help laughing.

"It's just a fantasy," she protested. "That doesn't actually mean I'm going to do it."

"So you don't think you'll ever go through with it?"

She shook her head. "No way. For me, a fantasy like that should just be a fantasy. Besides, I'm a virgin, and I won't lose my virginity until I'm married."

She smiled at the surprise on my face.

"It's a religious thing. I choose to honor it, but I also choose to use a very narrow definition of virginity."

"Ah, I see what you mean. Would you like to be my caboose, then?"

She wrinkled her forehead for a second, then laughed. "Yes, I'd be honored to be the last car on your taco train." She wriggled out of her tight jeans and then peeled off her black silk panties with a self-conscious look on her face. I eased her onto her back and spread her legs.

Her pussy was sweet and clean, with a spicy fragrance that suggested she had dabbed some perfume down there. I took my time, enjoying the feeling of being on my stomach rather than on my back, steadily bringing her closer to orgasm with a newfound confidence in my abilities. When she began to squirm and pant, I concentrated on her clit, sending her over the edge with a final swirling flourish of my tongue.

"Wow," she said simply, a few seconds later.

"Practice, practice."

She rolled onto her side, raised her head on her hand. "Let

me ask you, have you had any . . . relief tonight?"

"Nope. With me it's all give and no take. I just give and give and then give some more."

She giggled. "Would you like some take, for a change?" she asked shyly.

"God yes."

"Okay, you just lie still and let me take care of you."

I lay on my back and stared at the ceiling in happy exhaustion as Amira unzipped my jeans and delicately extracted my cock. She crouched over me, her dark hair shielding her face as if by modesty. Her tongue was warm and soft, her motions tentative and unpracticed. She held my cock gently inside her mouth, like she was afraid of damaging it, and moved her head up and down in a slow and steady rhythm. In the state I was in, it was enough. I closed my eyes and allowed myself to drift along patiently with the sensation.

"Here it comes," I said.

Amira lifted her head and took over with her hand, stroking my slippery cock with a firm grip. I groaned and spilled out my load in a prolonged spasm of pleasure. When it was over, the room seemed to be spinning in lazy circles, and I felt drugged. I lay there limply while Amira cleaned me with a towel and zipped me up.

"You're an angel," I said.

She smiled. "If my mother could see me right now, she wouldn't think so."

The next morning I was hung over, sore, and vaguely depressed. Instead of leaving me fulfilled, the escapade sent me into a funk that lasted for weeks. I remember thinking that Amira had it right—it was much better to let a fantasy remain a fantasy, and to remain true to your morals.

I called up Amira a few days later and asked her out. She

turned me down, politely but firmly, which only reinforced my feelings for her. I obsessed over her for a while, and then I eventually came to my senses. Still, I was shocked when, a year later, I heard that she was dropping out of law school because she was pregnant.

Today I look back at the incident with a strange mixture of distaste and pride. Should you act out an extreme fantasy when you have the chance? You're asking the wrong guy—I still haven't decided yet.

WADE KRUEGER
That's Awful, That's Nothing

Up on deck for a smoke break, we'd taken up the topic of aggression between brothers. It was the four of us: Birnauer, Hampton, Foster and I. A homely bunch of E-1s off the coast of Crete, our first Med cruise. The talk was charged with the heat of masculine competition. To have suffered the most under a brother was to have an edge on the others. Plus, we'd decided to make it interesting. Whoever won, we'd buy him drinks the whole time on the island. It had been decided, for no particular reason, that I should go first.

"My brother had access to sausage," I said. "Not patties but links. He worked in an Italian place. He'd bring home great long hoses of meat."

"What I wouldn't give for some sausage," said Hampton.

"Fry it up in a big black skillet," dreamed Foster. "Poke it with a fork."

"My brother would wait till I was asleep," I went on. "Asleep or passed out drunk. He'd sneak into my room with a foot's length of sausage and prod with it at my face. He'd talk to me the whole time. 'Won't you nibble on it? Little love bite? Lick the tip. Just lick the tip, that's all I ask.' I'd wake up with splotches of grease all over my cheeks and chin. I'd stink of paprika all day long. One drunk night, I took the sausage from him and clasped it to me fiercely. I held it like a teddy bear. He had to get pictures. He made duplicates, put the shots in everyone's locker at school. Even my girlfriend's. She could never look at me again."

"That's awful," Hampton said.

"That's nothing," said Foster. "My brother hit twelve and went crazy for jerking off. He'd take hour-long showers and jerk it three or four times. He was a regular jizz factory. You could never get it all out of the tub. He'd clog up the drain with it. I'd find little rubbery filaments of his spunk all over my ankles."

"I never went in for doing it in the shower," I said.

"Oh I did," Hampton said. "Still do. Bet I've used more Pert on my cock than my head."

"One time," Foster was saying, "I had to get in there. Had to brush my teeth. I had a date. I picked the bathroom lock with a coat hanger. He knew I was in there. Didn't care. The whole time in the mirror, I could see his silhouette through the curtain. Oh, he was working it. *Milking* it. Talking to himself the whole damn time: 'Getting close now. Getting close! Getting *close!*' He was keeping me up on his progress. By the time I'd rinsed and spit, he was saying, 'That was a nice one. That wasn't too bad.' Out on my date, I couldn't think about anything else."

"That's awful," I said. I knew I was out of the running.

"That's nothing," said Hampton. "My brother's cock is enormous. Got me by a good two inches, at least. I'm talking length and girth. Two years younger than me, walking around with the stuff of legend up under his Wranglers. From the time I got to where I knew how important your cock is, I knew what it was like to feel inferior because of my own. I understood how impressive his cock was before he did, and all I could do was envy the thrill he'd feel on finding out for himself. Lord, when he found out. He got laid more than I did. He did it with girls I wanted to do it with, and did it with some girls I even *had* done it with."

"Hard to believe there was a time in my life," Foster said, "I thought the thing was only for pissing."

"I get to where I think the pissing mechanism's only incidental," I said. "That just doesn't seem like the main work it's intended for, you know?"

"Situation similar to yours," Hampton said, indicating Foster with a nod. "Only worse. He was in the bathroom, I needed in. Only he didn't have the door locked. I just walked on in. He was stark naked in front of the mirror with that monster in his hand. He wasn't even hard. He just had it in his hand. He was flapping it, seeing how far up and down it'd swing. I got in there and he turned so he could show me. 'That's where it is,' he told me. 'That's where it is, and all Hawkinsville knows it.' It was like one of them snake handlers over in Alabama. I just turned and ran."

That one gave us pause. Hampton stood back with a smug look of achievement. "That'll be hard to beat," I said at last.

"That's awful," Foster agreed.

"That's nothing." Birnauer, whose idea this had all been in the first place, sucked his Winston to the filter and threw it overboard. He threw it like he was throwing a dart, like he had to aim at what he hoped to hit. Then he shook another from his pack and fired up. "Lemme tell y'all what I dreamed the other night," he said. He gave us each a look. "I dreamed I fucked my brother. He had a pussy, and balls too. I took him from behind, like dogs. Like I used to take my girlfriend, the one in Charleston. He made serious grunts and kept his eyes closed. He had a frown of pleasure on his face. He needed a shave and his skin wasn't so hot. Little breakouts here and there. When I came, I woke up, and goddamn it all if I hadn't soiled the sheets and jizzed in my shorts. And I'm not even queer. I don't know if I'll ever talk to him again. I've barely been able to eat for three days."

None of us had looked him in the eye while he was talking. None of us was looking at him now.

Then Hampton piped up. He knew it was over, but he wasn't going down without a fight. "You ain't sticking by the rules. Your brother ain't *done* nothing to you. That's all in your mind. That's something you done to your*self.* That's another contest. That ain't the game we was playing."

But we weren't the kind of guys to make much of technicalities. I made a move to go back below deck, and I was glad to have lost.

ROSALIND CHRISTINE LLOYD
Deflower

The Union Square Green Market has a certain nuance that cannot be found anywhere else in the city. New Age farmers gather there to hawk agriculturally sophisticated organic perishables and flora. It was early April and the sun was burning the New York City sky at an unseasonable seventy-five degrees.

A trough of wild orchids: their cups were tiny with colors so vibrant they seemed surreal. After I'd selected a nice bunch, while I was waiting patiently to pay, someone's elbow, sharp and swift, violently found its way into my left kidney. Now, I'm what's called a typical New Yorker. In other words, this rude, ill-mannered culprit was about to feel my wrath in the most scathing criticism I could hurl. I looked at the guilty party. Before me was a tight little ass squeezed into a pair of sinfully soft leather jeans. Bent over, this goddess stretched long golden arms sparkling with a thin film of sweat reaching over bouquets of flowers to retrieve her target. Choosing a wild rose a certain shade of pink so luminous it was almost fuchsia, she raised the flower to her face, allowing the silky petals to caress her nose. Satisfied, she cupped the bulb within the palm of her left hand, her long dainty fingers tenderly stroking the external smooth petals. I wasn't exactly prepared for what she did next. With her right hand, sinking her long finger into the corolla of the flagrantly pink rose, she penetrated the bulb while her left hand squeezed the silky petals. In a split second, every conceivable part of me capable of becoming aroused was demanding some serious attention.

Severely chiseled cheekbones cradled dark and sultry bedroom eyes that were opened only halfway as if in a perpetual state of arousal. Her short, naturally bushy spirals were streaked in brown and gold hues. Her skin color, glistening in the sunlight, reminded me of Grandma's hot buttered biscuits. Tall and thin, centuries of African royalty seemed embedded in her dignified posture. Full breasts were giving her ultra-tight T-shirt a hard time.

Seemingly content with her selection that included the pink rose, she thrust the bunch at the farmer. I couldn't believe her nerve. First, she assaulted me, then she molested a defenseless flower, then she jumped in front of me while in line. Strangely, instead of feeling angry, her aggression was turning me on. The farmer handed the roses back to her, wrapped simply in a thin sheet of tissue paper tied with sisal. My gullibility expected eye contact with her when instead, she slammed her entire body against me: breasts, thighs, mounds of Venus, all crashing together creating this confused exchange of energy so fast and hard it rattled me, making my head spin. The wind knocked from me, my orchids were tossed to the ground as "Leather Pants" marched on.

"I think she likes you," the farmer remarked, gathering my orchids and wrapping them for me.

"I don't think so. She practically knocked me over, " I answered, attempting to regain my coolness because my body was vibrating with both pain and pleasure while I watched her escape.

"Well, she asked me to give this to you." In his hand was the fateful molested rose.

Lingering behind her at a safe but interested distance, I watched as she browsed through a few veggie stands before darting across the street and into the Coffee Shop, a trendy restaurant on the Square.

Once inside, I didn't see her. Where could she have disappeared to that quickly? With flower in hand, I followed my feminine instincts and went directly to the ladies' room.

The door of one stall was open. I could hear a steady tinkle penetrating the ice cold water in the bowl of the toilet. She stood facing the tank as I peeked in, the toilet seat up, her magnificent naked ass exposed like an epiphany. Her leather pants were down around her knees as she straddled the toilet bowl. Ms. Thing was peeing standing up as if using a men's urinal—a woman after my heart. As she finished, without turning around she said, "Don't just stand there, come in here and lock the door behind you."

Standing directly behind this insanely beautiful woman with her pants down around her legs, I slammed the door shut, dropping my shoulder pack and flowers on the floor. Seizing her from behind, I wrapped myself around her like a depraved fiend. One of my hands fondled a breast quite warm to the touch. Arousal swept over me like a wildfire threatening to burn me alive unless I found something wet to put the fire out. While brutally swirling a pouty pierced nipple between my fingertips, my other hand went between her legs, dipping caramel fingers in between creamy thighs, sliding inside her hot, slippery wet cunt. My fingers manipulated her inflamed, pulsing clit sheathed in silky moist splendor, causing her to grind her bare ass into my crotch in a very demanding manner.

Balling my hand into a nice grip, I gently buried my knuckles deeper inside her flooding sex, deftly and steadily, stuffing myself so far into her that she whimpered, saturating my hand with soft heat.

Her hands were spread out in front of her against the wall behind the tank as if under arrest. With her legs spread open over the bowl, I reached for the fateful pink rose. As I glided it across her divine ass, a trail of goose bumps appeared, inciting more of her groans. Tenderly sticking the tip of the long stem of the flower in between her cheeks, I guided the rose downward as if arranging it within the confines of her beautiful juicy ass turned exotic vase, thorns pricking her tender skin in its trail. She sucked in bits of air between clenched teeth before moaning sensuously as I continued to slowly slide the flower in between her buttocks until the bottom of the stem appeared from her ass. When I carefully pulled the stem down from underneath her, the rose snuggled tightly between her ass cheeks. This rocked her, making her quiver and forcing her to whimper a little louder. I grabbed her mouth to muffle her. When she succumbed to silence, I licked the back of her neck with cat curls of my tongue. She tasted like salt, body lotion, and almond soap, making me wonder what her other wonders tasted like. My licking turned into fevered sucking, which caused her entire body to slide around in my arms as if begging me for something. After wiggling the long stem of the rose from between the divide of her ass, I lightly brushed its petals along the pretty tiny red imprints left by the thorns, taking broad strokes that gradually developed into a brief round of light spanking. Her sighs provoked me to guide the stem forward between her thighs, massaging the silky petals against the delicate flesh of her smooth shaven lips. We soon discovered we couldn't exploit the moment any further—someone entered the bathroom, going into the stall next to ours.

Gently removing the rose from between her legs, I got myself together, sticking the rose in with my orchids. Repressing the urge to take a playful bite of her ass, I allowed myself one final nibble of her luscious neck before picking up my shoulder bag, unlocking the door, and disappearing, leaving her surrendered over the toilet.

In hindsight, I think she learned a valuable lesson about disturbing flowers.

CHARLES FLOWERS
In This Corner

The first time I saw him was in the inaugural issue of *Sí,* a glossy magazine aimed at Latino readers. Fashion, language, food, music, bilingual education—all the concerns of middle- to upper-middle-class urbanites of Nueva York, Miami, Houston, Los Angeles. In the midst of all this culture was an eight-page spread of somebody called Oscar de la Hoya, a young boxer on the cusp of fame.

Oscar looked at me with his deep brown eyes and I felt my heart shudder: trouble. His face was pretty, with small features, lashes curling up toward his thick eyebrows. He wasn't a Tyson, some massive body of violence; he had a lean torso and a scattering of hair across his pecs, which were small but firm, human.

The first photo featured him in a deep purple satin robe,

shadow-boxing an imaginary opponent, the gym outside the ring dark and moody, broken by shafts of skylight. In the next shot he wore a midnight-blue satin shirt, open to his flat belly, his face wet from a spritzing. Another shot displayed him shirtless, leaning back a bit, his face lifted toward a fan circulating the sweaty musk of the gym, his hands thrust into linen trousers. I imagined him suited up, cruising Ocean Drive in Miami, wearing sunglasses, his face inscrutable, until a sudden burst of light: his smile, a crescent of white above his unshaven chin.

Transfixed by his stare, I was disappointed to find no real text to accompany the photographs, just designer names and prices. I didn't even know then if he was really a boxer; maybe he was just a model. Surely this perfect face had never been punched, bloodied. Boxers were brutes: Rocky, Tyson, Spinks, huge, ugly mugs of sneers and sweat, streaked with cuts and swollen with bruises.

But this boy was different.

⑥

Oscar. Not the most romantic of names. The Grouch. The Odd Couple. Oscar Mayer, aha, at last a pun, Oscar's meat, a phallic lunch-punch. But *de la Hoya* is another ball game, and my mind plays with the music of all those syllables, my toya de la boya. Delicious de la Hoya. All Day de la Hoya.

Once I began to look, Oscar was everywhere. His face was plastered all over town on posters advertising an upcoming bout. I'd come up out of the subway at Times Square to find an HBO billboard with DE LA HOYA emblazoned six feet high in golden letters. His fight face—no smile, concentration defining his brow—was fierce but still stunning: the same deep brown eyes, his slicked-back hair the color of asphalt wet from rain, sleek and shiny. I wondered what his fuck face was like. Framed by the wings of my legs, would he grunt and grimace as sweat dripped from his nipples onto my chest? Or would his face remain a mystery as he bit his lower lip to keep from smiling?

Cruising by a newsstand, I stopped when I saw him on the cover of *Men's Fitness*. As the reigning Welterweight Champion of the World, he was elected "Boxer of the Year" for 1997. The article gave all his career stats (27–0, 22 knockouts), which bored me, but then I started to stiffen at a photo spread of Oscar's workout tips.

After throwing money at the cashier, I raced home to draw a hot bath, my favorite place to masturbate. Soaking in near scalding water, I fed myself images of Oscar working out in his gym, his chest straining to lift a military press, his hands a blur as he worked the speed bag. As I licked at the sweat streaming down my biceps, I could taste the salt of his body, each bead of water wrung from his golden brown skin. I threw the magazine off to the side, then lifted my legs to my chest, clenching my knees as I sank back and down to the bottom of the tub. As I held my face up to the surface of the water, my lower back loosened, opening my ass to Oscar's liquid heat.

When I finally emerged from the bath, I found the magazine ruined, Oscar's body like mine: wrinkled and puckered in the steam. I resolved to buy another one the next day for a keepsake; in the meanwhile, though, at the end of the article I found a golden glove: *www.oscardelahoya.com*.

I logged on, dripping at my desk, and Oscar's home page flashed before me: a photo collage of Oscar, fighting, relaxing, smiling, sweating. I gorged myself with details from the interviews: a native of East Los Angeles, he was the only American boxer to win a gold medal at the 1992 Summer Games in Barcelona. Born in 1973, he lost his mother to breast cancer when he was eighteen. His father was a professional boxer in Mexico who pushed his young son to fight as early as five years old.

But a tenderness emerged that sounded all too familiar. When he first tried boxing, one of the profiles shared, he would cry and run home to hide in his room because he didn't want to fight. "A handsome young man with no steady girl-friend who is focusing all his energy on his boxing." His recipe for "Golden Blintzes" appeared in a Tito Puente celebrity cookbook. He rebuilt a run-down boxing gym in his old neighborhood, giving inner-city boys a chance at self-esteem and a career like his. And again, "A bachelor who dates often but has no steady girlfriend."

Cooks, does volunteer work, no steady girlfriend: sounds like the stories I told my family when I was in the closet.

That night I joined Team de la Hoya, his fan club. Four weeks later, for $39.95, I received a black baseball cap, a poster of Oscar dressed out in an electric-blue sweatsuit, a license plate frame (too bad I don't drive a low-rider), and a steamy, autographed portrait of him in black and white, wearing a black satin robe, his hands gloved and held up, the hollow of his chest a dark thicket of hair.

This lasted me for a while. Soon every Latino boy I passed on the street was a stand-in for Oscar, and I'd sniff as they passed to catch a whiff of cologne. My head would turn at every salsa tune drifting from a passing car. Riding the sub-way, I'd stiffen at the sight of a gold chain on a brown neck next to me, and I began to wish I were a crucifix to nestle in the black, wiry bramble of a Mexican boy's chest.

But it wasn't enough. I'd become a boxing junkie and a Latinhawk. When the Blue Velvet Boxing Club opened a few blocks from my apartment, I knew what I had to do.

⑥

I spent a couple of days walking by the plain wood storefront, trying to glimpse the shadowy figures within. I wanted to know what it felt like to box, to enter a ring with a man who wanted to hurt me. What would that do to my body? Besides, Oscar had inspired me. He'd given me an idea for a novel, an Anglo-Latino homo thang, like a gay *West Side Story. Oscar and Charles.* Boxer and editor. I wanted our lips locked in Latin rhythms, our tongues to tango across our borders. How could I write a convincing boxing novel, I rationalized, without training at a boxing gym?

I practically fell into the place. The door was old and creaky and jammed, so when I forced it open, I lost my balance and stumbled into a guy who looked like a manager.

"Whoa, buddy, what's up?" he asked.

"I wanted to find out about some boxing lessons."

"You've come to the right place. I'm Geno," he said as he offered his hand and then put a brotherly arm across my shoulders. "Let me show you the place."

His arm was heavy on my neck, but sexless in a straight-guy way, graceful and unconscious. His skin was smooth, pale olive, his dark hair oily. He smelled like fresh-baked bread, doughy and warm. He walked me around the ground floor, where a boxing ring sat majestic beneath the room's single skylight. Downstairs was a weight area, a locker room with showers, nothing fancy.

I nodded and tried to butch it up a bit, walking stiffly and deepening my voice, talking in monosyllables: "Cool." "Great." "Tough." The language of the enemy.

I signed up for a three-month membership and a set of ten training sessions, beginning the next day. I walked home exhilarated and terrified. I'd never thrown a punch in my entire life.

That night, in another hot bath, I thought of Oscar and wondered if my boxing lessons might lead to a chance encounter. Maybe I'd enter an amateur boxing contest and he'd be the judge. And I'd impress him, despite my rough skills, with killer determination. My will to triumph would inspire him to take me under his wing, and he'd offer to let me work with him in his training camp. Working out with him, running trails in the woods near his camp, sparring with him alone in a dusky gym, we'd grow close. He'd mentor me with his body, and ever the willing, grateful pupil, I'd offer my heart in exchange.

When I walked into Blue Velvet the next day, my chest fluttered, like the first time I dared to enter a gay bar. Geno threw me a towel and told me to pick out a locker downstairs. Undressing felt unreal. Whenever I'm naked in a new place, I get hard. When the air hits my skin, instead of getting goose bumps I stiffen, as if at any second I'm gonna get stroked. Undressed, my body became alive, expectant, even though the locker room was deserted. The newness of the place and the rhythms of the gym above made me feel even more naked and alien.

Upstairs, sexy disco music and testosterone were pumping at equal levels. There were a couple of guys working out in the ring, their bodies aflame with speed and sweat, throwing punches in time to the George Michael tune blaring from the speakers. I kept wanting to dance, but I was afraid I would move my hips too much.

"Yo, Charlie," Geno yelled as I walked up the stairs from the locker room. "Did you bring your wraps?"

"Wraps?" I had no idea what he was talking about.

"Never mind. Here, use these." He handed me two rolls of cotton material. "This is Ness, your trainer."

Ness was big—bigger than Oscar, who's only five ten and a welterweight (147 pounds). This guy looked like Tyson, a real heavyweight. His arms were massive hammers, and his navy T-shirt strained against his chest, the white Blue Velvet logo taut between his pecs.

"Hey, what's your name again?" he asked as Geno walked away.

"Charles."

"How 'bout I call you 'C'?"

"Sure." I thought, *Whatever.* "And you, your name . . ."

"Ness, as in Eliot."

He walked me to an empty area in front of a huge mirror that covered almost the entire wall. Off to my right was a Latino guy who looked about fifteen. He was boxing his reflection, moving and throwing punches to the beat pulsing from the speakers in the corners of the gym.

"First, you gotta warm up," Ness instructed as he led me through a series of squats and jumping jacks. Then he handed me a jump rope. "Do two rounds of rope, and then we'll put on some gloves."

My first thought was, *This is the test for fags.* Ness turned away, and I looked above the mirror at the wall, where the owner had painted ALL THINGS ARE POSSIBLE. I took a deep breath and threw the rope over my head. I tried to sort of run in place and not skip to Whitney Houston, who was belting out "I'm Every Woman." I managed to keep the rope moving for about five or six rotations—with girlish double-dutch chants going through my head—before I tripped myself. Ness was talking to Geno and pointed to a ringside box with three lights—green, yellow, red. The Bell. I soon learned that The Bell runs continuously whenever the gym is open. Like a traffic cop, The Bell dictates the gym's movements: three minutes of action (green), one minute rest (red). (Yellow means thirty seconds left: better throw your punch!)

After two rounds of rope, I nodded to Ness, who sat me down and said, "Give me your hand."

I held out my right hand; he took it and then spread my fingers apart. He unfurled one of the cotton rolls Geno had given me and began to wrap my hand. It felt odd to have his big brown hand take my pale pink one and gently wrap the material—stronger than gauze, more like swaddling—between my fingers and around my wrist and across my palm. Ness explained that wrapping hands is crucial to protect the knuckles. As he wove the cloth between my fingers, stopping occasionally to test the tightness of the layers, I felt shy, as if we were on a first date.

His grip was firm but, in a way, delicate, which surprised me. He finished with my right hand and began with my left, and again, tenderness mixed with the heat I could feel coming off his body. He was preparing me, and once more he warned me about getting the wraps right: too loose, he said, and you can break your own hand throwing a punch.

Then Ness showed me how to stand like a boxer, at an angle, with my left foot planted firmly before me and my right foot skewed. You have to keep your knees slightly bent, he told me, so you can bounce easily and swerve quickly. Hold

your right hand clenched and raised as if you're holding a telephone. Keep the left hand before you, as if to pound on a door.
Both hands hover at eye level, ready to jab forward into the
face of an opponent or to deflect a blow to the head.

"Now punch it," Ness said, holding up a padded red glove
that looked like a catcher's mitt. I threw my first punch, a left,
straight ahead into the red glove. *Phap.*

"Good. Again."

Another left. *Phap.*

"Good. Now give me a right."

A right hook is a harder punch, because the right hand has
to travel farther across the space between two boxers in order
to connect. It's a complicated move that involves turning the
whole body and churning power up through the legs so that
the body becomes a spring, coiled with force.

When I threw the right hook, my feet scraped the floor and
my hip lurched, throwing me off my balance. I stopped mid-
move when I realized I had fucked up.

"Naw, man. You gotta turn, move your hip into it. Like
this." Ness pantomimed the punch and raised his padded
hand right to my face. "Pow," he said, "like that, turn your
whole body into it. Now do it."

I repeated the punch until he said stop. I got better with
each repetition. My body learned the move, my foot shifted
stiffly, my hip turned, my right arm crossed the space between
us, all for that connection with the red pad: *Phap.*

"Okay, C, let's do a jab, then a hook, one-two, one-two, like
when you fuck."

Ness held his hands low in front of him as if he were grip-
ping a pair of hips and gestured fucking. One-two, in-out. He
grinned as he was doing this, and I couldn't believe the raw-
ness of the move. Surrounded by men hitting leather bags or

clinging sweatily to each other, he stood in the middle of it all and pretended to fuck the space in front of him. Before he could think, *This white boy can't even fuck,* I started doing it too, but with my arms throwing the punches.

"That's it, C, you got it." He grinned at me. "Now let's go."

I tried to forget that I was in a room of men, that there was violence going on not only around me but inside me. I found myself bobbing to the disco beat, hypnotized by the repetition of the punches, exhausted by each endless three-minute round. And I was amazed: I was throwing punches, I was hitting Ness's padded hands, I was hitting him as he moved across the floor. I couldn't believe I was hitting something, and it felt good to connect, leather against leather, when my knuckles struck his pads hard and direct. Sweat was dripping down my forehead; so I wiped my face with my arm. My hands were clubs—I had to hit something, anybody. Ness was grinning, leading me on, trying to fake me out with his own moves. The less I thought about what I was doing, the better I got.

Maybe that's what I was after: a body that worked without thinking, without remembering what to do, a muscle moving through space. I tried to imagine the two of us circling each other in bed. Who would top? Who would bottom? Already I felt how boxing becomes sex, the heat of two men moving in need, thrusting and sparring, arms locked in embrace—how in that haze of muscle and sweat, everything else drops away, the two bodies the only reality.

But I couldn't block out the surroundings: the weighted bags, the mirrors, and, especially, the other boxers as they moved through their workouts. Mostly black or Latino, they were young, fierce, and focused, pounding the heavy bags or sparring with partners. As Ness and I wove across the floor, we brushed against punching bags and sleek, wet bodies. I leaned into their heat, shimmering like a horizon all around me. I'd glide against a sweaty black arm or bump up against a brown leather bag, my sweat leaving a trail across the room.

By the fourth or fifth round, I was totally drenched with sweat. During a rest minute, Ness got a water bottle from a cooler by the ring. I started to take the bottle from him, but he gestured for me to lean back and open my mouth. He shot the water into my mouth, then all over my face. He squirted more than I could swallow, and the water washed over my chin and down my chest. I dropped my head and he continued to pour the cool water over me, soaking my head, as I stared down at the drops hitting the floor.

"Awright, man, that's it for today."

He led me through a cool-down of push-ups, crunches, and squats, and I did as he commanded, counting under my breath, silent and sweating, doing whatever he said.

Downstairs, alone again in the locker room, I sat on the single bench and felt the blood rush through my body. I stripped and stood in front of the floor-to-ceiling mirror. I was dripping with sweat, and my limbs were pink and bright. I grabbed my right biceps and was surprised at its hardness. Is this what "pumped" felt like? I felt leaner, meaner, and I wondered what Oscar would have thought of my body. Did I have what it takes to be a fighter? Was my body a weapon? What things could it do?

As I entered the shower, I could hear the music from upstairs, the clear note of The Bell every three minutes. I imagined Ness up there, working on another boy, turning him into a man, a machine of muscle and speed. Maybe it was all about contact, the touching, the way Geno draped his thick arm around my neck, the way Ness wrapped my hands, then showed me how he fucked. Maybe what I wanted from Oscar was his touch, the pummeling he could offer—what touching him, even in violence, would mean for me.

The water was hot, adding to the heat of my body as the blood stayed near the surface of the skin. I lathered my chest with soap, then foamed up my groin. I was hard, my balls as tight as the speed bag upstairs, which I imagined a Latino boy pumping with his fists. I started to jerk off, my rhythm copied from the boxers I had watched, one-two, one-two, finding a rhythm and letting my body take over.

When the bell sounds, Oscar approaches me from across the ring, the EVERLAST of his red satin shorts all I can focus on. I can't look at those eyes yet, but I can see his red gloves hovering before me. I take a defensive stance, then begin circling him. He throws a left jab, which I block, and his lips protrude over his mouthpiece, like a child pouting. My hook catches him off guard, my glove grazing his chin. His hairy chest damp with sweat, he moves closer, and I back away. He follows me as I dodge his punches, trying to gauge how long I can last before he hits me again.

Backed into the corner of the shower, all I hear is the slap of leather against muscle—hard, then gone. My fist curls around my shaft, one-two, one-two. I back away, but he's there, leaning into me, dancing me into the corner, where I'm all his, and I bite into my lips to draw blood to spit in his eyes. I can see his fists coming at me, and I want to break that smile that's haunted me. His hands are on my ass, spreading my cheeks apart as he plunges all the way into me. His strokes are hard and quick, and he leans into the spray to kiss me. He pumps harder, never taking his mouth from mine. We breathe like swimmers, gasping whenever our tongues break the surface of the water pouring over us.

As he fucks me harder, my cock swells. Pinned to the tile, I'm up against the ropes, and he continues to pump me harder and harder. I hold my arms up to defend myself, against his chest crushing me, and I am stroking faster and his look is fierce, his brown legs spread wide as he squats and rises, drilling me into the corner. His right hook against my thigh, his left jab pounding my pec, I'm twisting against his blows and the sweat blinds me, his face a blur, water and salt and hair against my lips. His voice comes from the water, *Sí, ahora, sí, ahora,* and he bites his lower lip, his perfect shining white teeth like a tourniquet he loosens, releasing his jism into me. When I shoot, the cum hits his chin, but before he can lick it away, the water rinses him clean. He opens his mouth like he's about to sing, and what comes out is the language of men fucking men: syllables wet with heat, a cry opening into water.

Upstairs, there were new faces as I moved toward the door. Pulling my sweatshirt over my head, I almost ran into a young Oscar, maybe eighteen. He was warming up, stretching, throwing a few punches at a bag, and he looked at me from the corner of his eye. If we had been in a gay bar, I'd have considered it a cruise, but in this place of sweat and leather and muscle, it was more a leer of competition, checking me out. Am I tough enough? Am I tougher than he is? I wondered what would happen if we stepped into the ring together: who would throw the first punch, who would be left standing, who, perhaps, knocked cold.

HANNE BLANK
And Early to Rise

To your way of thinking, it isn't morning until the sun comes up. Even then sometimes it isn't, for you are loath to admit the coming of a new day until you've determined that you are ready to be a part of it. I have known you to spend entire mornings, even into the afternoon, lying in bed with your laptop computer, working on some part of your dissertation for hours with the curtains still drawn. Eventually you emerge, as bleary as if you'd been sleeping all the while. "Beautiful morning, isn't it, Lilja?" you call cheerfully into my study as you stumble toward the shower, sometimes as late as two o'clock, finally condescending to formally enter the day.

And so for your sake I will say it was the middle of the night, despite the clock on the bedside table that gleamed a red and resolute 5:45 A.M., when I awoke to find you waiting,

silently wanting, your back slightly arched, your areole crin-
kled, still fast asleep. Thank God you don't dream of sex every
night, you tell me, since it always frustrates you when you do.
Always the bridesmaid, never the bride, you say, you never do
get what you want in those dreams, and you wake frustrated,
slippery between the legs, softly grumbling. I can always tell
when you've dreamt of sex. In my study I hear you through
the wall when you shower, leaning against the tile with the
water pummeling the lush breasts I like so much to tease, your
hand between your thighs, unaware that the shower actually
does precious little to cover your noises. I listen to you, something deep between my hips quivering at the high, piercing
whimper that I know means you're hovering, aching and desperate, at the edge of orgasm.

I wish I weren't such a morning person, wish my body
didn't always insist on my being awake so long before you.
This morning—morning for me comes when my body says it
does, circadian jackboots kicking me rudely awake even if it's
December in New England and still dark as the hem of a cas-
sock—I began to wake, yearning to just roll you over and slide
between your legs but not daring to rouse you just for that.
You slept deeply, though, and in the depths of your slumber
you seemed to welcome the caress of my hands, letting me
spoon you cozily, my palm sleeking the fine full curve of your
hip and drifting over the pillowsoft of your belly. Stirring
slightly but not waking up, you seemed to know I was there,
and for a while that was enough. And so I pressed myself
against your spine, my nipples perking slightly at the contact
with your skin, slid my arm under the graceful arch of your
neck. Unconscious kitten-murmurs came from your throat as
my fingers traced the seam where my thigh pressed the back of
yours, and as I let my hand meander to the top of your thigh

there was a slight, unmistakable shifting of your hip pressing into my fingers.

Wondering whose hands caressed you in your dreams, wondering where you were and who she was and whether you could see her face as her hand moved where mine did, I smiled at your reaction, experimentally pushing my knee against the backs of your thighs to see if you'd let me push your legs apart. I flattened my palm against the top of your breastbone to hold you steady, to keep you pressed against me. You arched a little, letting me spread your thighs, those thick gorgeous thighs I love to knead, to stroke, to kiss, to taste, not legs so much as feasts, as succulent and resilient to my bites as grilled sausages, yet as sweet and satiny as ganache against my tongue. Suddenly I could smell the wilderness of your aroused cunt and realized that yes, I was right, you had to have been dreaming of sex even before I began to touch you. I wondered how far you'd let me go, how much of this I could enjoy before you woke and shooed me away, protesting *auf Deutsch,* too agitated and asleep to remember how to scold me in English.

Hands moving slowly, not wishing to disturb your lust-saturated slumber any more than absolutely necessary, I found a nipple with one hand while the other inched its way between my leg and yours, pushing against the sleek flesh to either side. Your nipple was crinkly, hard, the tip of it already sensitized to the touch of some imagined seducer's hands. With the pad of a finger I circled it, traced it, outlined it, imagining each ridge and whorl of my fingerprint rasping against it like corduroy, fantasizing that in your sleep, your normal sensitivity would be perhaps enhanced to feel it. Your breathing shifted slightly, deeper now.

I love, have always loved, will always love, entering you from behind. There is an almost illicit thrill in reaching just below the lavish halves of your ripe peasant ass to find the hidden hot-velvet cornucopia of you, lips thick with blood and pouting, poised, waiting to be kissed, parted, spread, entered, gorged beyond rational thought or even the rhythm of breathing. I teased your pussy as we lay together in the softness of the pillow-banked bed, two fingertips grazing just inside your lips where the skin is moist to the touch. Your mouth opened, breath still regular and slow, still asleep. My hand moved above your breast, letting your nipple rumblebump against each finger in turn as I fanned my hand to and fro.

When you are awake, you won't often let me tease you like that for long. You become too impatient, begin to urge your hips backward against my fingers, start grabbing at your own breasts, greedy baby, needing the pinch of thumb and forefinger on those hardened tips to sear through your body and spike the need building behind that anxious clit of yours. Not now, though. Did my touches become the touches of the lover in your dream? I hope they did. I wanted to do you that way, the dream way, slow and deliberate, the kind of teasing that leaves you so wet and frustrated that you have to exorcise yourself under an entire water heater's worth of hot water, not stopping until the goose bumps are too severe for you to bring yourself off again. Would it embarrass you to know that I know how you fuck yourself with the hair conditioner bottle when it's worse than usual, when the dreams have made you need it deep and relentless but you still can't bear to admit to wanting to be fucked quite so hard? You never ask me to come back to bed when you wake up like that. It makes me jealous, usually. But not this time.

Did you notice, in your fevered sleep, that I had begun to push inside you, or that you were slick as egg whites? I wonder at what point it began to register somewhere in your hindbrain that someone else's hand really *was* forcing its meaty way inside your clinging, slippery folds. There was no resistance as I entered you, sweet rippling girlflesh opening around my fingers. A momentary ripple of worry seized me—would you take it as a form of rape if you woke suddenly to find me coaxing three fingers inside of you without your knowledge or say-so? It troubled me, but the more I thought, the more the thought curled in on itself and became redolent with even deeper, redder lust. *Would* I violate you? Yes, in a manner of speaking, I would, I would take the blame for having wanted this so much that I would do it to you without asking, because I knew it was the only way I would get to do it at all.

Tender violent thoughts circled, tail in mouth, in my brain. Creator and destroyer, I cradled you in the gentle curves of my protecting arms, against the softness of my body, wanting to be as brutal as I was loving, to ruin you with the force of your very own desire. My fingers searched within your cunt, trembling, wriggling, in and farther in to you, almost shaking with the effort not to go too fast, not to blow my cover, not to wake you too soon. I wanted a sudden, rough, raw, overamped fuck like the one we had on the first night we did it, when our bodies screamed for each other like the angst-driven guitars onstage at the club where you backed me up in the corner behind the speaker stack and bit my neck and told me you wanted to take me home with you so you could bend me over in my miniskirt and shove your tongue into me. You told me later that it cost you a good deal to restrain yourself until you'd gotten me into your apartment before you shoved your fingers into me, pinning me against the wall, reaching without preamble under my skirt, shoving past my panties and making me arch and groan out loud with the outrageous desire to feel you there, so rude and yet so pure. It cost me at least as much in the dark hours of this early morning not to do the same to you, not to slam-fuck you into the bed with sharp corkscrewing strokes, not to bite your bubblegum tits until you screamed, not to shake you awake with the rude force of unbounded lust.

With a slow spiraling motion your hips moved, sluggish, the burgeoning energy of the fuck drawing you toward me. Your pussy opened a little to take me in, and I distinctly heard a foggy moan muffled against the pillow. I plucked your nipple: *she loves me, she loves me not, she loves me, she loves me not,* letting my fingers slip off of the tip before they could pinch hard enough to puncture the bubble of unconscious arousal in which you were still, somehow, sleeping. Twisting my wrist a bit, I began to knead the resilient walls of your cunt, a sensation I know you adore, reading the braille of muscular twitches, the occasional contraction, the opening-up just at the tips of my fingers that made me suddenly wish I could cum into you like a man, fill that space with the essence of myself so that it would ooze out of your cunt later and remind you where I'd been.

She loves me. Wrist gliding to the left, my fingers arched, stroking up and over, finding the firm nubbled spot where you like to feel my first knuckles rub. *She loves me not.* To the right then, my fingers bent double, doubly thick, feeling you spread your legs reflexively, opening to me, your cunt stretched around me, almost but not quite a fist. *She loves me.* You rolled back against me, pressing your ass hard against me, sweet sensation having woken you slightly. *She loves me not.* I let you turn onto your back, shifting with you so that I didn't have to stop fucking your voluptuous sleepy cunt. You seemed not to mind, not even to be surprised, that you woke with my fingers inside you: you wanted it as much as I thought you did, my intrusion not only tolerated but welcomed with a short soft cry. Reaching up as I settled on my belly between your sloppily splayed, sleep-limp legs, I plucked your nipple again. *She loves me.*

You hovered somewhere just this side of sleep as I straightened my fingers again to reach farther into you. You've always liked me to stroke the scalloplike slickness of your cervix with my fingertips, the sensation so deep, so intense and primal, that hidden bit of you found out and gently burnished as if such polishing could make it shine like gold. My fingers swimming through the honeyed heat that had begun to seep out of you and trickle down along my wrist, you moaned, beginning to arch toward me in a slow agonized rhythm. I looked up at you, your hands on your breasts, fingers splayed, mauling your own soft flesh with the same insensible heartlessness with which your cat, in similar states of bliss, will knead her pin-sharp claws into my thigh while I cringe and keep on petting her.

It was time to finish your dream the way I'd often wanted to, to be the one to take the place of whoever had begun to seduce you as you slept. I parted your labia with my lips and nose, tongue extended to stroke its way to your clit. At the taste of you my own cunt clenched, and I think I moaned against you as I found your hard sweet clit and fastened my lips around it, fingers still swirl-kneading the very bottom of your muscular cunt. Your hands abandoned your breasts and made a basket around the back of my head, holding me as I licked you, up and up and up against your clit, the motion I know will get you to come and come again if I keep at it, if I fight you after the first time when you try to push me away. Starving for the taste, the feel, the sound, the clinging grasping arch of you at orgasm, I battered your clit with my tongue, making no pretense at subtlety. Mashing my face against your soaked pussy, you ground against me with an agonized sound and I tried to lick faster, wishing my mouth into a blur of spit and muscle to please you.

You made the noise, and my clit throbbed in sympathy. *The* noise, not just any noise, not to be mistaken for any lesser sex cry. In the nineteenth century it was believed that the Bird of Paradise had no legs and thus could never land, that it had to fly the heavens forever in its shockingly extravagant robe of feathers. Is that why your cry sounds like some fantastic bird, because of your desperation to land and your inability to do so quite yet, from the sudden realization that the plumes of sensation are not enough when you begin to writhe from having flown so hard for so long? Your breath came in gasps, your muscles taut as harp strings, shuddering, and I rammed into you hard, dropping gears suddenly into the kind of all-out fuck I'd wanted to give you all along. You made the noise a second time and groaned, hoarsely begging me please, please.

Your throat went rigid with a soundless scream, an outraged howl tearing through you as I fucked you hard and harder, eating your clit with toothscrapes now, knuckles mashing against the entrance of your clasping hole with each stroke. Somehow you caught one enormous gulp of air, but I wasn't ready to let you come down yet. I nudged that infamous spot inside you with my fingertips, Morse code telling you to come for me again, again, again, tongue lashing at you as insanely as I could. You had to come again, my fingers insisted, one more time, for me. Your fingers left my head and I knew, as surely as I knew you would only come for me again if I forced you, that you were twisting your own nipples far more cruelly than I ever would have, enchanted past the point of pain by merciless need.

Come for me, I willed as I felt you tensing again, come for me. I pistoned my hand in and out of your dripping cunt, jackhammering you well beyond the point you thought you would not reach again. The first one was for the dream. The second was all mine. What came after that was yours and yours alone, until you simply could not, and lay dazed and sweat-damp in my arms.

The sun was just barely up, the day bluish-gray at the corners of the curtains. Pulling the covers back up over you, I bent and kissed you as you lay there, spent and sleepy, eyes glazed. You stroked the side of my face and smiled a little weary smile. I kissed your palm and you blushed, looking amazingly like the pictures I've seen of you as a little girl.

"You're getting up now?" you mumbled, letting your eyes close again.

"Yes, baby. Time for me to start the day."

"Nnnpfth. *Schrecklich*. Morning people." Your grumbles grew more distant with each syllable.

"Go back to sleep," I replied, "it isn't morning for you yet."

"Mmmmmmphh," you sighed in agreement as you rolled over, cocooning yourself in the eiderdown, already asleep again. I stood and walked toward the door, licking my lips to savor the taste of you. How pleasantly ironic, I smiled to myself as I walked naked down the narrow hallway to the shower, feeling my clit burning with quiet impatience, on my way to revisit the juncture of wakefulness and dream.

JACK MURNIGHAN
Rooster

My wife is dead; with her dies all the guilt, most of the joy, all the wonder that remained. Dead, she's like a hole in my memory, or like a light that shines on everything but itself. What's my mind doing to me? Most the time it's hard even to remember her face, but damn if I don't remember the ones before, the one during. Only one; seventy-one years and only one other. I had been married to Eve for what seemed like forever and then there she was, like a flake of hot fire dropped out of the sky. So innocent and unsuspecting, with eyes made to paint sadness on and an ass that made you want to take her like you take a calf for branding. God, I was double her age plus eleven; no business pulling off those cotton pants with all the damnation that lay beyond. Life's a shitkicker, all right; all those years faithful as an anchorite and then that. What is a man? Someone who plucks or someone who doesn't need to? Not sure I'd want to be the one any more than the other. I knew Eve knew, knew she smelled that girl on me just as I did, even after all the soaping. Wasn't even that there was anything to smell, just that when I touched my wife it was like I had gloves on, like a film had settled over my fingers so they'd advertise their little infamy. Tried to hide it that night by tonguing her two times to the end—probably gave myself away right there. Women always know when you're enjoying it, and when you're just doing it out of guilt—you learn that after a while. I remember the first time I went south on a woman: pulled her out behind a grain silo and down in the mulchy field and had her knickers at her ankles like I knew which fucking end was up and how to make out all the messages my pecker was trying to send me. She kept saying Lick it, lick it, and no way was I about to ask for a little explanation so I just put my whole face in there, put it in there just like an armless man would eat spaghetti. And that's how I felt, all armless and handless and eyeless, just a nose and a tongue poking around, trying to get a sense of things. I came to like it, thought it was kind of my secret weapon. It wasn't like sex, where some men treat the thing like a ten-trial Olympic event while others do it like they were punching a time card. Kissing pussy, it's more like you can't really do a bad job—like Christmas or something where just the intention is good enough. I'd tell those farm girls that I was gonna eat them out like a dog cleaning a can. And they'd let me all right. I think that's why all the married ones liked me so much: their own husbands had long since stopped trying, didn't give out none of the preferred love and sometimes didn't even stick it to them either. Always felt like I had that up on other men; they just let the days pass by, didn't even think about how a little here and there would make all the difference. Other men's wives taught me how to be with mine. I remember one who'd get me to come over, hog-tie her with my belt, tell her all kinds of nastiness and fuck her like the war was gonna start up again tomorrow. Jesus. Ninety-four years old and I still don't understand women. Don't know what they want but to feel like they're beautiful and to have you think their cooking's good. My Eve, she was about as capable in the kitchen as she was in the master bed. Never did tell me till after her fiftieth year that she'd been dreaming of me taking her up the behind. Just imagine, my wife of thirty years, telling me she wanted it all along. And there I was like some kind of idiot greasing up my cock and sticking it this way and that way, and what with all the Vaseline it kept sliding into her cunt and she's saying Like this honey, like she'd thought about it so long she'd know where I was supposed to put it to get the damn thing in. It didn't seem that different to me, kinda like stroking it with your left hand instead of your right—the feeling is there, but you don't quite know what you're up to anymore. And it was kinda funny seeing Eve, all fifty-two years of her, bunched up on her knees, face pressed against a pillow. Laughter ain't always a good addition to sex so I was keeping myself quiet. And she kept saying Is it good for you, honey, is it good? And I think I said Yes, yes, so many times it might well have been the best I'd ever had. But it wasn't. It was Eve and it was always Eve and that's what I thought was good. Men fantasize about a lot of shit—this playmate and that actress—but over and over I'd be inside her thinking This is my wife. My wife. This, right here, is my wife. She'd suck my cock and she'd be my wife. She'd ride high up on me, cross bouncing on her bosom, and she'd be my wife. She knew I had wronged her, knew I was weak, and all those years didn't say word one about it. And so when she asked me to take her there, even when I poked once a bit too much and hurt her, she was my wife, and I knew she loved the god-all of me. I don't think there's a way of telling someone that what you love about them is just that they are. But that's how it was. I just wanted to say You you you, over and over till she knew I loved her. Then she died and it wasn't even like part of me, no, it was just that they took away my colors, took away my leaves. I seen an oak one time strong enough to grow its way through a link fence. That's what she was to me. Grown up and through me like I wasn't even there. Now I'm an old man and it don't suit me to cry. And I make my way. Ain't nothing but women here in the home, and each of them saying I'm their Georgia peach. Not even that I'm any kind of man, just the idea of a man to them. So I help them with their baths—assist them, as they like to say—and call them all Sugar like they're the only one, and Ingrid gives me her dessert because she's Watching her figure, and May likes to put a hand on my thigh, and Chlora just goes on and on about What a fine-looking man I am, but she says her grandson is fine looking too and he looks about like a woodchuck. Day to day, I'm the little rooster in the hen house, kissing all the bearded ladies. Eve, where are you Eve? Why did one of us have to go? I told you I'd never leave you and I never will. You used to say Where's my man, and I'm here, honey. I'm here. Goddamn it, I'm still here.

Contributors

WENDY BECKER is a Ph.D. student in California, where she studies lesbian representation. When she's not writing about lesbian desire, she's studying it in her seminars or enjoying it in her bedroom. Her work has appeared in *Hot & Bothered 2* and *Best Lesbian Erotica 2000.*

DODIE BELLAMY is the author of *The Letters of Mina Harker, Real* (with Sam D'Allesandro), and *Feminine Hijinx,* as well as several chapbooks, including *Cunt-Ups.* She lives in San Francisco with writer Kevin Killian.

TODD BELTON is a writer by avocation and a programmer by necessity. He lives with his fiancée and two cats in the wilds of Greater Boston, writes about seven thousand words a week for various Web sites, and knows the location and exact contents of every single fetish fiction page on the Web. "Expanding on an Idea" is part of an ongoing series, which can be found at www.inu.org/twentysix.

HANNE BLANK is the author of *Big Big Love: A Sourcebook on Sex for People of Size and Those Who Love Them,* editor of *Zaftig: Well-Rounded Erotica,* and associate editor of ScarletLetters.com. Her online pied-à-terre can be found at www.hanne.net.

CARA BRUCE is the erotic editor of Libida.com. Her short stories have appeared in many anthologies, including *The Oy of Sex, Best Women's Erotica 2000* and *2001,* and *Best Lesbian Erotica 2000.* She edits the Web zine *Venus or Vixen* (www.venusorvixen.com) and is the editor of *Viscera: An Anthology of Bizarre Erotica.*

NATHAN ENGLANDER is the author of the collection *For the Relief of Unbearable Urges.* His stories have appeared in *The Atlantic Monthly, The New Yorker, Story, The Best American Short Stories 1999* and *2000, The O. Henry Prize Anthology 2000,* and *The Pushcart Prize Anthology XXII.* Born and raised in New York, he has been living in Jerusalem since 1996.

CHARLES FLOWERS is the director of marketing and promotion at the Academy of American Poets. He received his MFA in poetry from the University of Oregon, and he is the coauthor of *Golden Men: The Power of Gay Aging.* "In This Corner" is his first piece of erotica, and he hereby offers to take on Oscar de la Hoya, anytime, anywhere, as long as they can shower together afterward.

DAMIAN GRACE. a scientist who lives in the Chicago area, has been writing erotic fiction under the name DG for four years. Many of his stories can be found on free Web sites sprinkled throughout the Internet. He enjoys getting feedback and can be reached at DG@newsguy.com.

GINU KAMANI has been asked whether she is from Afghanistan, Bengal, Bolivia, Brazil, Chile, Ecuador, Egypt, Ethiopia, Fiji, Goa, Gujarat, Guyana, Hawaii, Iran, Iraq, Israel, Kerala, Maharashtra, Mauritius, Mexico, Pakistan, Peru, Puerto Rico, Punjab, Spain, Trinidad, Turkey, and Venezuela. She is the author of *Junglee Girl* and lives in Northern California.

WADE KRUEGER is a student in the creative writing MFA program at Ohio State University. He was raised in Georgia and visits regularly.

TSAURAH LITZKY's work has appeared in three previous editions of *The Best American Erotica,* as well as in *Penthouse, Paramour, Pink Pages, Longshot, The Unbearables, Help Yourself,* and many other publications. She teaches erotic writing and erotic literature at the New School in Manhattan. She believes this is the Promised Land.

ROSALIND CHRISTINE LLOYD's work has appeared in *Hot & Bothered 2, Skin Deep,* and *Pillowtalk II,* and will also appear in *Set in Stone* and *Faster Pussycat.* Currently travel editor for *Venus* magazine, this womyn of color, native New Yorker, and Harlem resident lives with her unruly feline, Suga, while obsessing over her first novel.

JOE MAYNARD moved in 1981 from Nashville to Brooklyn, where he has since been happily observing his navel grow larger with each beer. He also publishes *Beet* and *Pink Pages* and writes for *The American Book Review* as well as previous editions of *The Best American Erotica.*

DAN TAULAPAPA McMULLIN lives in San Francisco and Samoa. His screenplay *Bikini Boy* is under option with Kunewa Productions and in development with the Sundance Native Screenwriting Program; it was produced onstage at Theatre Mu and Soho Rep. He has performed at the New Zealand International Arts Festival, the Pacific Festival of the Arts in Samoa, Highways in Santa Monica, La Peña in Berkeley, the Walker Art Center in Minneapolis, and on TVNZ in Aotearoa (New Zealand). His stories and essays have been published by Bamboo Ridge, Cleis Press, Wasafiri UK, Colors, Folauga, Resistance in Paradise, and Penguin. He was the NEA Millennium Artist-in-Residence in American Samoa for the year 2000.

JACK MURNIGHAN is the editor of *Nerve* and also of the recent anthology *Full Frontal Fiction.* His weekly *Nerve* columns on the history of saucy literature, "Jack's Naughty Bits," will be released as a book in May 2001. He has a Ph.D. from Duke University and a BA from Brown University. He lives in Manhattan's Chinatown, ever on the prowl for cheap eats.

MARGE PIERCY's most recent novels (of her fifteen) are *Three Women, Storm Tide* (with Ira Wood), and *City of Darkness, City of Light.* Her most recent poetry books are *Early Grrrl* and *The Art of Blessing the Day.* She has given hundreds of readings, lectures, and workshops.

M. J. ROSE's novel *Lip Service* was first discovered as an

e-book online in March 1999 and was picked up by the mainstream publishing industry. It was chosen to be a Featured Alternate Selection by the Doubleday Book Club and Literary Guild. Since then, it has been published in six other countries. Her new novel is *In Fidelity*. Rose has also coauthored *How to Publish and Promote On Line*.

DANI SHAPIRO is the author of the novels *Playing with Fire, Fugitive Blue,* and *Picturing the Wreck,* and of the memoir *Slow Motion.* Her work has appeared in *The New Yorker, Granta, Story, The New York Times Magazine,* and many other publications. She teaches in the graduate writing program at the New School and lives in Brooklyn with her husband and son.

JERRY STAHL is the author of the narcotic memoir *Permanent Midnight,* which was made into a movie starring Ben Stiller. His second book was the novel *Perv—A Love Story.* He lives in Los Angeles.

MATT BERNSTEIN SYCAMORE is the editor of *Tricks and Treats: Sex Workers Write About Their Clients.* His writing has appeared in *Best American Gay Fiction 3, Obsessed, Flesh and the Word 4,* and other publications. He is currently working on an anthology, *Dangerous Families: Queer Writing on Surviving Abuse,* as well as a collection of short stories.

CLAIRE TRISTRAM (www.tristram.com/claire) is a freelance journalist living in San Jose, California. Her short fiction has been published recently in *Alaska Quarterly Review, Fiction International, North American Review, Massachusetts Review,* and *The Best American Erotica 2000.*

JAMES WILLIAMS's stories have been published in *Advocate Men, Attitude, Black Sheets, Blue Food, International Leather- man, Sandmutopia Guardian, Spectator,* and other magazines, and in anthologies such as *The Best American Erotica 1995, Bitch Goddess, Doing It for Daddy, Guilty Pleasures, My Biggest O,* and *SM Futures* and *SM Visions.* He was the subject of pro- file interviews in *Different Loving and Sex: An Oral History.* He lives in the San Francisco Bay area.

Reader's Directory

ARSENAL PULP PRESS

Arsenal Pulp Press is a leading independent press publishing a wide range of titles, which include *Carnal Nation: New Sex Fictions; Exhibitions: Tales of Sex in the City; Quickies*: *Short Short Fiction on Gay Male Desire*, volumes 1 and 2; and *Hot & Bothered: Short Short Fiction on Lesbian Desire,* volumes 1 and 2. For more information, write to 103-1014 Homer Street, Vancouver, BC, Canada V6B 2W9, or visit www.arsenalpulp.com.

AUNT LUTE BOOKS

Aunt Lute Books is a multicultural women's press publishing original fiction, nonfiction, and anthologies. Contact Joan Pinkvoss, senior editor, P.O. Box 410687, San Francisco, CA 94117, or visit www.auntlute.com.

CLEAN SHEETS

Clean Sheets is a free online erotic magazine, updated every Wednesday. It showcases erotic fiction, poetry, and art, as well as provides information and commentary on sexuality and society. Editor in chief: Mary Anne Mohanraj. Fiction editors: Kristine Hawes, Jaie Helier, and Bill Noble. Publishing weekly since October 1998 at www.cleansheets.com.

CLEIS PRESS

Cleis Press celebrates twenty years of publishing smart, provocative books on sex and gender by authors such as Gore Vidal, Pat Califia, Susie Bright, Tristan Taormino, and Carol Queen. Cleis Press, P.O. Box 14684, San Francisco, CA 94114, (800) 780-2279.

THE FLESH AND THE WORD SERIES

Obsessed, edited by Michael Lowenthal, is the fifth volume of the best-selling *Flesh and the Word* series of erotic anthologies featuring explicit, unflinching, confessional memoirs from the best gay writers in America. The collection includes work by Scott Heim, Andrew Holleran, Allan Gurganus, D. Travers Scott, and many others. For more info on *Flesh and the Word* volumes, see www.penguinputnam.com.

INTERNATIONAL LEATHERMAN

The preeminent magazine of the gay-male leather/SM/fetish scene, *International Leatherman* offers authentic leathersex and edgeplay in every bimonthly issue. *Leatherman* includes commentary and discussion from respected members of the community, erotic leather fiction and photo layouts, "how to" articles, a leather calendar, and personal ads. Published by Brush Creek Media; edited by Jim Hunger. Subscriptions are $39 per year. Write to Brush Creek Media, 2215-R Market Street, #148, San Francisco, CA 94114; www.brushcreek.com.

NERVE

Nerve and Nerve.com are print and online magazines of exceptional photographs and writing about sex and sexuality for both women and men. *Nerve* publishes Pulitzer Prize–winning authors alongside MoMA photographers, causing *Entertainment Weekly* to call it "the body of *Playboy* with the brain of *The New Yorker.*" *Nerve* has published three books to date: an anthology from its first year, *Nerve: Literate Smut;* a fiction collection, *Full Frontal Fiction;* and a photo collection, *Nerve: The New Nude.* *Nerve* will be publishing a history of sex in literature, *The Naughty Bits,* in summer 2001. Visit www.nerve.com.

PHILOGYNY

Philogyny is published by PussyWhipped Publications in Boston. It is a print zine (back issues are available). Contact Philogyny, P.O. Box 381732, Cambridge, MA 02238, or philogynyzine@hotmail.com.

PINK PAGES

Pink Pages is the best erotic magazine in the five-borough area. A sample copy is $2, a subscription is $5 for three issues; subscribers must provide age statement with correspondence. Please note that *Pink Pages* is published infrequently. Write to Pink Pages, P.O. Box 879, New York, NY 10021-0002.

POCKET BOOKS

Lip Service by M. J. Rose was published in hardcover by Pocket Books in 1999 and in trade-paperback format in 2000. Readers who enjoyed *Lip Service* will be pleased to hear that M. J. Rose's new book, *In Fidelity,* is arriving this year. Pocket Books is a division of Simon & Schuster, the publishing operation of Viacom, Inc. Visit www.simonsays.com.

THE WALRUS

The Walrus is a national literary review and is published annually by Mills College. It is an all-encompassing anthology, spanning all genres of writing. To get submission guidelines or to purchase individual issues, please write to *The Walrus,* c/o Mills College, 5000 MacArthur Boulevard, Oakland, CA 94613.

WILLIAM MORROW

William Morrow is an imprint of HarperCollins Publishers. *Perv—A Love Story,* by Jerry Stahl, was first published by William Morrow in 1999. A general-interest trade publisher, William Morrow has published *Boy Island* by Camden Joy, *The Herbert Huncke Reader* by Herbert Huncke, and *The KGB Bar Reader,* edited by Ken Foster.

Credits

Reader Survey

1. What are your favorite stories in this year's collection?

2. Have you read previous years' editions of *The Best American Erotica?*

3. If yes, do you have any favorite stories from those previous collections?

4. Do you have any recommendations for *The Best American Erotica 2002?* (Nominated stories must have been published in North America, in any form—book, periodical, Internet—between March 2000 and March 2001.)

_____

_____

_____

_____

5. How did you get this book?
_____ independent bookstore
_____ chain bookstore
_____ mail-order company
_____ library
_____ sex/erotica shop
_____ borrowed it from a friend

6. How old are you?

7. Male, female, other?

8. Where do you live?
_____ West Coast
_____ South
_____ Midwest
_____ East Coast
_____ Other

9. What made you interested in *The Best American Erotica 2001*? (Check as many as apply.)
_____ enjoyed other *Best American Erotica* collections
_____ editor's reputation
_____ authors' reputations
_____ enjoy "Best of"–type anthologies
_____ enjoy short stories in general
_____ word-of-mouth recommendation
_____ read book review

10. Any other suggestions? Feedback?

Please return this survey or any other BAE-related correspondence to: Susie Bright, BAE-Feedback, P.O. Box 8377, Santa Cruz, CA 95061.

You can also fill out this same survey online at www.susiebright.com/movies/bae01.html.

Thanks so much; your comments are truly appreciated.